WILDFLOWER

by David Cox

ALSO BY DAVID COX

NOVELS

The Old Must Die

Petrarchan Girl

Fearful Farewell

COLLECTIONS

Faded

Split

SCREENPLAYS

Student Loaners

Return of the Devil

Curmudgeon

#Anhedonia

NONFICTION

Indie!

This is a work of fiction. Names, characters, places, and incidents are either the product of the author's imagination or are used fictitiously. Any resemblance to actual persons, living or dead, events, or locales, is entirely coincidental.

Slain Diamond Books

Copyright 2022 by David Cox

All rights reserved.

Printed in the United States of America

For Mom

"God bless our love

two branches of one tree

face the setting sun."

Grow Old with Me, John Lennon

PROLOGUE

One Wish

"I hate movies."

Mom looks over at me. She is a good-natured person and it shows outwardly, but when she is tired, she is less able to hide her more negative emotions. I can tell she is annoyed with me, just the slightest bit. "I'm not asking you to watch a documentary," she says. "Just something… fun."

"What did you have in mind?" I sigh.

"Well, first, I thought you should make some coffee for us. I love when you make it."

"I don't feel like I make it any differently."

"No, you do. It's a lot stronger than mine. Perks me up."

"I think you just like my coffee because I'm the one making it."

She smiles. "That could be it, too."

"Alright," I chuckle. I walk into my parents' kitchen and prepare a "strong" pot of coffee, as requested.

"Make sure you do a full pot!" I hear her yell from the other room.

"Ok!" I holler back. Nothing my mom does really *annoys* me, especially during this past year or so, except for one thing – her "hollering" voice. It goes right through my ears. Sends me directly back to my childhood. But I'm not about to make a comment about it now. Instead, I close my eyes, breathe in slowly through my nose, exhale meditatively, and then add in more scoops of ground coffee. I press start on the machine and then walk back into their living room.

"Coffee's going," I say. I look over at their massive TV. "Dad really got the biggest one they had, didn't he?"

"You know your father," she says, half good-natured and half-irritated. Moms always say "your father" when they're irritated – not "my husband."

"So what are we gonna watch?" I ask. "If I'm going to sit in one place for an hour or more, it needs to be something really good. It needs to hold my interest beyond a couple cups of coffee."

"You didn't like the movie last week?" she says with a fake frown.

"Yeah, I did," I smile, unable to lie. "I'd never seen it before, but I guess that isn't saying much."

"Oh, stop it," she says. "You have too."

"No, I think I'd remember it," I reply as I squint to try and remember.

"You don't remember watching *What About Bob?*"

"Not at all."

"We watched it all the time when you were a kid. All four of us."

That must be why I don't remember. I don't remember many times when the four of us were actually all together in the same room. She must be more confused than I thought.

I do not let Mom into my insights, though. She has been paranoid lately about losing her mental capacities, so my version of the story would only upset her. "Oh, yeah, maybe I do," I lie.

She nods, thankful that I finally came around. "I was about to say…"

"Today, though?" I ask again.

"I thought we should watch *Cape Fear*," Mom says, with a smile that's a tad sinister. She has a dark side that is mostly enabled through horror films.

I feel my face scrunch up again. I can't help it. "Isn't that a black-and-white movie, though? With the dude from the hotel-ax-killing movie"?

"What are you talking about?" she asks. "Jack Nicholson? *The Shining*?"

"Is that who that is? He's all crazy and stuff in the movie."

"Which movie? *The Shining* or *Cape Fear*?"

"Uh… both? I think?"

Mom stops to think. "Wait a minute, Em. Jack Nicholson was crazy in *The Shining*, yes. Well, he gradually goes crazy. But he's not crazy in *Cape Fear*."

"Are you sure?"

"Of course, I'm sure. He's not even in *Cape Fear*!"

"He's not? Are you sure?"

"Will you stop asking me if 'I'm sure'?" she asks, exasperated.

"I dunno," I say. "Like I said, I don't watch movies like the rest of you guys."

Mom closes her eyes and holds up a finger. "Okay, I think I got it now. You think Jack Nicholson, from *The Shining*, is in *Cape Fear* because he was 'crazy,' right?"

"Right."

"You're thinking of the wrong actor. Gregory Peck is in *Cape Fear*."

"Was he crazy, too?"

"No."

"So why am I confusing the two actors?"

"Because Gregory Peck was in *To Kill a Mockingbird*," she says with a sense of relief.

I stare, not connecting the dots. "Was he crazy in that or something?"

"No!" she laughs. "Jack Nicholson was in a movie called *One Flew Over the Cuckoo's Nest*."

I'm still stumped. "And he was crazy in that?"

"Yes," she says simply.

"So…?"

"So," Mom says, all drawn-out, "you're confusing bird movies – '*Cuckoo's Nest*' and '*Mockingbird*.'"

"Oh okay, so both actors are in movies about birds."

"No," she shakes her head, "the movies aren't about birds. They just have birds in the film titles."

"So why am I so confused?"

Mom looks at me, befuddled. I am not sure which of the two of us is more present at the moment. "Emma," she says slowly, "listen carefully. Jack Nicholson is in *The Shining* and in *One Flew Over the Cuckoo's Nest*."

"Okay. And he was crazy in both movies?"

"Correct. Crazy in both. Different kinds of 'crazy,' but still… Yes."

"That's odd. Was he, like, odd in real life or something?"

"No, he's just a good actor," she says. She then waves me off, trying to get back to her original point. "So, anyway, Jack is in those two movies. Gregory Peck – a completely different guy as you can tell by his name – is in '*Mockingbird*' and *Cape Fear*. You were just mixing up bird movies that have nothing to do with each other." She eases back into her chair after her summation.

"Okay, I think I follow now. So, Gregory Peck is in *Cape Fear*, the movie you want to watch today. Got it."

"Actually, he's not."

"He's not?"

She thinks and then says, "No, actually he is."

"He is?"

"You're thinking about the black-and-white version, which starred Gregory Peck. I am suggesting we watch the remake of *Cape Fear*, in which Gregory Peck has a small role. A cameo."

I nod my head slowly. "That's kinda confusing. And by kinda, I mean a lot confusing."

She laughs. "It kinda is."

"You want to watch the remake and not the original? Aren't the original versions of films always better?"

"Not always."

The timer on the coffee pot sounds. I stand up and say, "You want a full cup?"

"Yes, please," she says, grabbing the remote. "I'll get this ready while you fix our coffee. Two sugars and two spoonfuls of creamer, please."

"I know how you take it by now," I say from the kitchen. I pour and prepare hers first, and then I prepare mine – black with two sweeteners.

I bring the two large mugs back and hand hers over. I look at the TV as I sit down. "Martin Scorsese? I know that name."

"You should. One of your dad's heroes."

Oh, great. No wonder I knew his name. He probably talked more about him than he did me when *he was actually at home.*

Again, I withhold my negativity. "Okay, well, I'm ready when you are."

Mom starts the movie and I slide into the couch that hugs the long side of the room. I kick my feet up. Dad's recliner is actually the best spot in the room to see the TV, but I refuse to sit there. I would rather watch the TV from an odd, less advantageous angle. Mom never fast-forwards through the opening titles of a movie, so I *patiently* wait through them, only thinking about how three more minutes of my life are being pointlessly wasted.

A big orchestral sound kicks in as the title *Cape Fear* appears onscreen, followed by a pair of large eyes, underneath a watery surface (I'm assuming they're Robert De Niro's – I saw him in Netflix's cast list before Mom clicked "Play"). Just as the title card (I hate that I even know that term) appears, I hear Mom shout.

"What's the matter?" I nearly shout as well. Quickly placing my coffee on a side table, I rush to her. It looks as though she has spilled some of her coffee on her shirt. She quickly sets her mug aside, splashing it more as she does. "Oh, I know that hurts, Mom. I did that just a couple of weeks ago."

Mom starts crying. I freeze when she does, not fully understanding her reaction. I snap out of it and bend down to rest on my haunches. "It's okay, Mom, really. I'll go get…"

She puts a hand to her face to cover it. I know she hates crying in front of me, and she does all she can to suppress her tears when Steve or I are around. I have told her countless times that it is okay to cry in front of me, though. It's only natural. I would be crying all the time if I were her. In fact, I know she cries often, because when I pop by their house unexpectedly, I'll often catch her, eyes red and freshly wiped as she opens the door.

"It's not that," she says. She pulls out her damp shirt a bit and looks down at it. "I just got this."

Even though Mom is not able to go to church on Sundays anymore – or anywhere, for that matter, without a walker – she still dresses up just the same on that day. She wants to maintain her normal routines as much as she can, but those routines disappear more and more each week. Today, she is wearing a new red blouse and a pair of black slacks. The coffee has stained the bottom of her shirt.

I place my hand on hers. Normally her hands are very warm, but they feel colder today. "Mom, it's okay. Really."

She grabs me gently around my neck and pulls me in for a hug. She cries into my shoulder, letting herself fully break down in front of me for the first time in a long while. "I'm just scared," she whispers into my ear.

My eyes well up instantly, but I manage to keep my voice strong. "I know you are. But you're doing great. Plus, you have another appointment coming up soon, *and* we should be hearing back about those results from last week's scan any day now. Right?"

She silently nods, still crying. She then pulls away from me and looks into my face. "I'm just so worried."

I grab the remote and click the "Pause" button. "What are you worried about?" I ask. "I mean, right now, in this moment?"

"I'm worried that my mind is slipping... that my body is starting to fail me," she says, looking down at her shirt again. "The coffee just... my hand was shaking..."

I place my hand over hers again. Her trembling simmers a bit. "First off, your mind isn't slipping. You just schooled me in Film 101. I still don't know the difference between *The Shining* and *'Mockingbird'*..."

Mom groans.

"...and, sure, your body is going to act differently because of the radiation, but all of that is normal. You know that. It's all a part of getting better."

I pause and look her in the eyes. She searches mine for reassurance, like I used to do when I needed her to tell me I was going to be okay when I was scared to go to my first day of school or my first tee ball game.

"If you're *that* worried," I continue, "then I will do whatever I can to help you out. You know that."

She sniffs and her tears stop. "What do you mean?"

"Well, if you're worried about memory loss or something, we can read a book together. That way we can keep both of our brains engaged – together. Mine could use some fine-tuning as well."

"A book?"

"Yeah," I say, getting excited. "We could read a chapter a day, or however long it is between visits, and then discuss it the next time we see each other."

She perks up a bit. "What should we read?"

I think over some options. I am no literary expert, so I try to remember one I studied in school so that I can already be somewhat knowledgeable about it before walking into a book club meeting. Not only is that intimidating, but I want to be able to carry the conversation if Mom struggles to remember aspects of the story.

Definitely not Hemingway, though.

"What about a classic?" I suggest. "Like *The Great Gatsby* or *The Catcher in the Rye*?"

"Ugh," Mom groans. "I tried reading *that* one. So much language... The Lord's name all the time. Was that necessary?"

I think again and then suggest, "How about *Of Mice and Men*?"

Mom thinks it over and smiles. "Yeah, I think I'd like that."

"Great, I'll order two copies today, so we can start by the middle of this week," I grin.

Mom reaches up and hugs me again. "I'm sorry, honey."

"For what?" I ask, buried in her shoulder.

"For crying."

This time, I pull away. "You do *not* need to be sorry for that. I cry all the time."

"You do?" she asks, looking shocked.

"Of course, I do."

"About what?"

I stare in disbelief. "About you, Mom."

Now, she is shocked. "You *do*?"

"What am I, some kind of monster who doesn't care about her own mother?" I scoff.

"No, it's just... I don't want you kids to ever worry about me. I just want you to be okay. Always."

"Steve and I will always be okay. You don't need to worry about that." I rub her back once more before I release her and stand back up. "Now, can we stop being so grim? You *are* okay. You spilled some coffee. That's all. I ran over a squirrel on my way over here. No biggie. I certainly didn't cry over that."

"Oh, no. Did he live?"

I quickly think over my options in answering – *to lie or not to lie*. I decide to be honest. "I don't think so. He was kinda floppin' around when I looked in my rearview mirror. I just saw his tail kinda swirling all over the place. Definitely didn't look natural, even for a rodent."

That makes her laugh, which makes me happy.

"Hey, before we get started with this movie again, do you think you could help me get to the bathroom?"

"Oh, sure," I say. I grab her walker and place it in front of her. "Do you need me to help guide you or…?"

"No, nothing like that," she says. "I will need help with one thing, though."

A silence grows between us. I think I know what she means, but I am hesitant to say anything first, based upon her reaction to her spilled coffee.

Finally, I ask, "You mean you'll need help if it's… a *bowel movement*?"

She looks away embarrassed. "I need help wiping." She pauses. "But not in back."

"Oh. You mean…?"

"The front," she says simply.

I am struck speechless, but I know I need to help her out in any way I can – I just said that to her less than five minutes ago. "Y-y-yeah, I can do that," I say sheepishly, trying to act brave.

She stands up, holding onto her walker and then pushes my shoulder with a good amount of force. "I'm just messin' with you, Em," she says with the biggest smile.

I laugh hard. "You will never change, you know that?"

She laughs as she walks away. I carefully lift up her oxygen tube so it extends fully and doesn't get tangled on anything. When she returns, I retract the tube and place it next to her chair as she re-adjusts the piece under her nose.

I inspect her with one exaggerated eye open. "You sure you're good?" I tease her.

She smiles and then gives me another big hug. "Thank you, Em. I love you."

"I love you, too, Mom."

She grips me tighter before releasing me and gently setting herself down into her chair.

"I just want you guys to be okay."

PART ONE

Anywhere but Here

Two Weeks Later

1

"Hello?"

Even I know my greeting is barely audible, but the caller has no issue deciphering my voice through a pillow. There is only one person who can understand my incoherent, mumbly speech easily.

"Emma, it's Steve," my brother says. "I'm on my way over there now." He pauses. "Are you still asleep?"

I peer at my alarm clock and see that it is nearly eleven o'clock. "Nowehemnausilslepin," I answer, which he understands as, "No way. I'm not still sleeping."

"Okay, good. You better not be," he says, unconvinced.

"You have the birthday cake?" I ask with better diction, sitting up now.

"It's currently riding shotgun."

"You didn't get one with a number, did you?"

"Of course not."

"What's on it?"

Steve pauses and then replies, "Well, it's got stars, some swirly designs…"

"Red, white, and blue?" I ask, pulling my jeans up with a small hop. I can get myself together surprisingly quickly. It is, perhaps, my only truly great ability.

"As a matter of fact," he says slowly, "yes, it is."

"It's a Fourth of July cake isn't it?"

Another pause. "Crap."

"How could you not look more closely at the cake before you bought it?" I ask, agitated.

"I dunno," he says. "I just assumed... It's not my fault Mom's birthday is so close to Independence Day!"

"No, but it *is* your fault that you didn't do your *one* job correctly, which was to buy our mother a *birthday* cake," I say. I tussle my hair, hoping it will fall down in a decent way, as I look myself over in the mirror. *Eh, it'll do.*

"At least I'm not still in bed at noon on Mom's birthday!"

I quickly hit the FaceTime icon on my phone. Steve answers it. "You see?" I ask. "I'm not in bed. I'm literally putting my shoes on now," I say, as I point the camera down to my Vans as I slip them on. "And it's not noon yet. Exaggerator." I open my front door.

Steve groans, unconvinced. "Whatever. I'll see you in forty minutes?"

"More like thirty," I say as I start the engine of my car.

"Don't speed, moron," he says. "There's no sense in having two family members in the hospital."

"I'll be careful," I reply as I blindly back out of my driveway, nearly taking out my trash can as I do. Trash day was three days ago, but that's irrelevant at the moment. "Just go up to Mom's room. I'll be there in twenty-five."

With that, I hang up the phone and head to my mother's current residence – the hospital.

2

Twenty minutes later, I am in the hospital elevator. I hit the number "5" button and patiently wait. I find myself constantly rushing through my life lately – as my speedy arrival just demonstrated – but my life slows down, at least momentarily, when those metal elevator doors close. I have approximately twenty-two seconds to myself, and it is during these brief moments that I am able to collect myself and to try and slow my breathing. I have suffered from severe anxiety since high school, but it has only worsened since Mom's illness was discovered over a year ago. Once she was admitted to the hospital, though... Well, let's just say, I'm swallowing Xanies like they are mints left on a hotel room pillow.

Breathe, I demand. *Don't let your mind race. Clear your thoughts. Be strong for them.*

I take one huge breath, which is quite an achievement for someone who suffers from my ailment, just as the elevator doors open. I step out and peer around the corner and spot my brother.

"Have you been in yet?" I ask when I see he is still holding the cake.

"Not yet. They were doing some physical therapy when I arrived, so I waited in the lobby. They should be about done."

"What are they focusing on today?"

"Just walking mainly. She apparently did pretty well this morning. Barely needed help walking to her bathroom."

I look down at the cake. "Are you serious?"

"We already went over this," he barks out. "I don't want to hear it."

"Steve, the cake says, 'Are you *FREE* tonight?' and there's a picture of a bald eagle wearing stars-and-stripes sunglasses."

He sighs. "I understand that I made a mistake."

"You didn't even look at it before you bought it, did you?"

Another sigh. "No. That should be obvious."

"Are you still even willing to debate that I'm the favorite child?"

Steve laughs mockingly. "I don't think my cake faux pas erases her memory of your *entire* high school experience."

"Oh, well, excuse me, Mr. French. You act like you were perfect..."

"Compared to you, I was."

"You were much worse in college," I remind him. "I, at least, settled down."

"Settled down?" he scoffs. "Is that what you call it?"

"Careful what you say next, Brother," I speak slowly. "You may be older..."

"Yeah, I'm older, but yet you have *still* managed to have already been divorced twice."

I glare at him. "Those divorces were not my fault. I think you know that. Plus, need I point out that...?"

"Yeah, I've been divorced, too, but at least I only put them through that experience once."

"With a kid," I quickly add. "So... I win."

"You're such a bitch," he laughs.

If anyone else had said those words to either of us, we would have never spoken to that person again. That is the beauty of a sibling relationship. You can say whatever vile thing you can think of to win an argument, and there are no consequences. At least that has always been the case between Steve and me.

"You're all set to go in now," a nurse says cheerfully as she exits alongside the physical therapist.

"Everything seem OK?" Steve asks. He is always the one who talks to the doctors, nurses, and the other assorted hospital staff. I tend to shut down during social interactions with strangers. Or anyone. He may not be the best at picking out a cake, but I am grateful for his other abilities.

"Yeah, she is looking better this morning and moving pretty well," the nurse replies. "If you need anything, just push the button."

"Thank you," we say in unison.

He turns to me. "You ready?" We both then stare at the large wooden door before us.

I attempt to take another deep breath, but I am unable. I am cut short. This causes a small tick up in my anxiety. I know not to attempt another breath, because it will only cause my anxiety to worsen. Instead I try to clear my head. I look over my shoulder and then ask, "Hey, where's...?"

"Outside," Steve answers prematurely. "He's on the phone."

"For how long?"

Steve stops to think, but really, he is hesitating. He knows his answer will only anger me and create an inevitable future fight, and that is the last thing he wants on Mom's birthday. "Well, I'm not sure…"

"How long?" I demand sternly.

"Two hours. Based on when I texted him this morning and asked what he was doing."

I glare at him. "*Two hours*? What could possibly be…?"

"Nothing," he cuts me off. "Nothing is more important. We know that. But I think Dad's been offered a job."

"A job? He's retired!"

"You know how it is… you're only retired until you're desired again."

"Oh, yeah. He's desired all right," I sarcastically add.

"His stuff has been surging lately. Did you see that *Out of Mind* broke into Netflix's top ten? That's crazy."

"No, I didn't," I say unenthusiastically. "Could not care less. I hate movies."

"You only hate them because of him."

"Well, duh."

I hate movie with a passion – their phoniness, their run-of-the-mill plotlines, their bloated budgets, their preachy "messages," and their art-by-committee nature. Yet, despite my hatred, I know an inordinate amount about film. I can cite quotes, character names, and actors without even thinking. Why do I have this *unique* ability? Because I was indoctrinated by my father.

Essentially, I was brought up in the church of cinema. I'm like one of those kids who went to Sunday school every day for thirteen years and then became an atheist. Despite no longer believing in God, that person can still rattle off the first fourteen books of the Bible, the Ten Commandments, and the nature of the triad and deity of God with confidence. Growing up religious, whether it is in a church or a cinema, has long-lasting ramifications.

We both look at the large wooden door again. "Come on," Steve says. "Let's go wish her a happy birthday."

3

"Hey, guys," Mom says when she sees us. She slowly raises her left hand to beckon her children. "Come here, sit down."

Before we do, Steve and I both give her a kiss and an awkward hospital-bed hug. Each obstacle that deters my ability to properly show my affection becomes my enemy, and this bed is currently persona non grata.

"Happy birthday, Mom," I say as I lean back up from the bed. "And look!" I say, turning toward Steve, like I were a *Price is Right* girl.

"We got you a cake!" he chimes with a big smile.

"Aw, thank you guys so much." Mom cranes her neck to try and see the top of it. "What's…?"

"Oh, well, I know how you like birds and…" he quickly retcons.

Mom gives me a sideways glance. She birthed both of us, so she knows when we are trying to put one over on her. "It's a Fourth of July cake, isn't it?" she asks me.

"Yes, it is," I acknowledge.

"All of my life, I just wanted to have my own special day…" she says, feigning sadness.

"Mom," Steve pleads.

"I never could. I always had to share my day with someone else…"

"A whole nation," I quickly add.

"A whole nation of people," she continues. "It's easy to get lost in a country this big. Makes me feel…"

"Unimportant? Forgotten? Overlooked?" I suggest.

"Stop it!" Steve shouts, breaking into laughter. "I don't know how I could make this mistake year after year when you make me feel so guilty."

"If you feel guilty, then that's your own fault," Mom says. She then breaks character and waves him over again. "Come here, Stevie," she says, pulling him down for another hug. "You know I love you."

When Steve gets back up, he looks at me and quietly mouths "the favorite," which makes me break into a smile.

"You want me to cut you a piece?" he asks her.

Mom grimaces, and Steve and I both know the reason why. Our mutual joy dissipates. She has not been eating well lately. Mom wants nothing more than to go home, but to do so, she must start eating again. Soon.

"Did you have breakfast?" I ask.

"No, but you know how the food is here," she answers.

"We would be more than happy to bring you something," I say. She, of course, already knows this, but she has yet to take us up on our offer. She just simply does not want to eat, whether hospital imitation food or a gourmet spread is being offered.

"I know you would," Mom says. She looks over the cake again and then appeases us. "I'll take a *small* piece. Just don't give me any part of that eagle."

Steve smiles. "You got it." He grabs a plastic knife from her bedside table.

"Actually, should we wait for your dad?" she asks.

Steve and I exchange a glance. My eye twitches, which is his sign to take the lead. "Well, he's outside. Not sure when he'll be back up. He should be here soon."

"Oh," Mom says quietly.

My heart breaks as I see Mom's do the same. Apparently, it is not enough that she has to deal with stage four cancer – she also has to be married to a level ten jackass. But, as much as it pains me, I know I need to form a unified front with Steve when it comes to Dad – at least around Mom.

"Yeah, I saw him when I got here," I say. "He'll be up any minute."

Mom tries to smile. "Okay. Good."

Steve hands her a small piece of cake on a flimsy paper plate. I grab a spoon from her table and place it next to her slice. Everything about this makeshift party is making my emotions run wild inside. The plate, the utensils, the low sounds coming from the TV, the harsh light coming in from the window, the beeps of machinery in the hall… I feel nauseous. And angry. And sad. And defeated.

Mom looks at the small token of celebration on her plate and begins to cry softly. She is obviously trying to hide her tears from us – like she always does – but we both swoop in.

"Mom, it's okay," Steve says. "You don't have to eat if you don't want to."

"It's not that," she says, still looking down.

"You just want to go home," I say.

Mom nods as her sobs intensify. Her face breaks and tears fall. Struggling, she holds up both her arms and pulls Steve and me into another hug. We remain silent as she sobs but then collects herself. "I'm sorry," she says. "I try to never do that in front of you guys."

"We know, but you don't have to go through that added effort," Steve says.

"For real," I add. "We're sad, too. We've been sad for more than a year."

"I know," Mom says. "I just want you kids to be okay." She has rarely addressed even the notion that she may not be here with us in the future, so her words hit us hard.

"We will be," Steve says. "Let's just focus on getting you home."

"You're right," Mom says. She then looks the two of us over, admiringly. "I sure did make handsome kids," she smiles proudly.

"Em loves when you call her handsome," Steve says with a laugh.

"Steve does, too, because he never hears it anywhere else," I shoot back.

"I love you both," she says and she picks up her spoon, shaking off her children's nonsense. She scoops up the smallest bite of cake that she can manage and chews it.

"How does freedom taste?" I chuckle.

Mom smiles and continues to chew. After a moment, Steve and I instinctively look at each other. Something seems off. With that size of a bite, she should have been able to swallow that piece of cake whole. There was no need to still be chewing it.

"Make sure you get it all down," he says.

"Do you need a drink?" I say at nearly the same time.

Mom stops chewing and swallows. She looks around the room. Her eyes do not look confused, per se, but they look as though they are on a search mission.

"What's wrong, Mom?" I ask. My breathing intensifies as I feel my anxiety building to an insurmountable level.

"Mom?" Steve says. "Can you answer us?"

She mumbles slightly and we both lean in. "What did you say?" I ask. She mumbles again, more incoherently and softer. "Steve?" I blurt out, looking to my older sibling for guidance.

"I'll call the nurse," he says, shooting up from his chair.

I hear him on the intercom behind me, but he may as well be twenty miles away. I stare into Mom's eyes as their focus falters. I can feel her fear. I grip her hand. "Can you move your hand at all?" I ask her.

As the nurse enters, I hesitantly let go of Mom's hand, giving the nurse room to examine my mother.

"What seems to be going on?" the nurse asks us as she tries to speak, both to Mom and as an aside as well.

"She took a bite of cake and then just... stopped responding," Steve answers.

"No verbal response? What about body movement? Did she move her head or eyes toward you when you were speaking to her?" she asks.

Steve seems lost. "I, uh, I don't... No, I don't think so."

"We'll take her down for a CAT scan. We should have results within an hour or so." The nurse then calls her station as Steve and I share a quick worried glance.

I look down at Mom as her eyes continue to scan the room, never really focusing on any one thing. Despite being able to hear our worry just now, she does not seem to show any sign of fear of her own.

A doctor arrives and tells us he will be moving her downstairs for the test. He speaks to us nicely, but Steve and I know it is time to leave the room.

"We'll be back soon," Steve says to her, over the backs of the doctor and nurse as they prepare to move her from her bed.

I try to say "I love you," but my body locks up. I, too, have suddenly found myself speechless.

4

"What the hell's going on in here?"

Steve and I have been staring at the floor of the lobby, gathering our thoughts and trying to make sense of the current state of things, and hearing our father's loud, abrasive voice reminds us that things have not hit rock bottom yet – because he had only just now arrived.

"Hey, Dad," Steve says with zero enthusiasm.

"What's going on? I was gone for twenty minutes and now your mother isn't in her room."

"Twenty minutes," I scoff.

"Huh? What was that?" he barks.

"They took Mom downstairs to get tested..." Steve begins.

"Tested?" he interrupts. "For what?"

"We don't know. We were with her *while you were on the phone*," Steve says, laying some guilt on the last few words, "and she suddenly... stopped talking."

"What do you mean, 'stopped talking'?"

"What do you think he means?" I assert. "What else could that mean?"

Dad's lip curls as he weighs the decision to argue with me or to focus on the new series of events. Thankfully, for his own health, he chooses the latter. "How long?"

"They said an hour. Results should be back about any time," Steve says, dropping his head.

Silence overtakes the room. Finally, Dad seems to understand the severity of the moment. Somewhere in the background, though, I can hear Judge Judy yelling at a defendant. Our moment of quiet solitude is broken.

Oh, how I hate TV. Why must everyone always have a TV on? Is there anyone else alive who is willing to sit in silence for five minutes?

"Are you the Morris family?" a voice asks from behind.

We turn and see a new doctor. We have met so many that it is impossible to remember their names. I have to go by their looks or ages if I want to recall any of them.

Steve replies, "Yes, we're here with Annie Morris, awaiting results."

"I have them," the young doctor says. He grabs a nearby chair and pulls it close, completing our circle. "It seems as though Annie has suffered a stroke," he continues. He speaks softly and empathetically, but the words coming from his mouth make his voice sound every bit as abrasive as my father's. "Actually, she has suffered several strokes, but the one she suffered this morning was the biggest and most severe."

"A stroke? Several of them?" Steve says aloud, trying to understand.

"That's right."

"How long until we can take her home?" Dad asks with a furrowed brow. We are all shaken by this news, but Dad's comment shows just how oblivious he is to her recent downward turn in health. "Her physical therapy was going well. They said she might even get released today."

"Unfortunately, this changes things," he says. "We won't be looking at a release today."

"I've got to get her home," Dad continues. "She doesn't want to be here. She hates it here."

"I understand completely. That's also why I wanted to speak to you all directly. I think it would be a good idea to have a 'family meeting' today. Just to discuss options. Would any of you be opposed to that?"

"Options?" Steve says. He looks at Dad and then me, but we are still in a state of shock. "Yeah, I think we could do that. Is that okay with you? Dad? Em?"

I nod as Dad mutters, "Yeah, sure."

"Good," the doctor concurs. He looks at his watch, and I cannot help but think how long it has been since I have actually seen a person wear one. It is in moments like these that I find myself noticing the odd things about life that seem out of place. "Let's see, it's almost two o'clock now. How about we set up the meeting for three o'clock? That okay?"

We all nod.

"Okay," he says, rising. "I will see you in about an hour then. Room 540."

"A stroke?" Steve repeats, once the doctor is gone.

"Several of them," I say, shaking my head.

We are all so confused. This is not what was supposed to happen. Today is Mom's birthday. She was supposed to go home. That was her "big gift."

I look up at a clock on a faraway wall. The minute hand has barely moved past the twelve. The clock seems frozen in place. Dead.

"How can time move so fast and so slowly at the same time?" Steve says, looking at the same clock. Our sibling powers seem to be aligning once again.

"This was not supposed to happen today," I say.

5

"Sit anywhere you'd like," a social worker tells us as she opens the door to Room 540.

I enter first and look around. It is an odd room. There is a couch, two recliners, a rocking chair, and a table with some office chairs around it. On the wall are framed scenic paintings, and, in the corner, is a bookshelf with assorted books about grief and faith. It is only after seeing that bookshelf that I feel my anxiety uptick again. *Something's off.*

Not really knowing what to do, I decide to sit in a recliner. Steve follows me and sits on the sofa, which is the nearest spot to me. Dad sits on the sofa as well, making sure to sit on the opposite end to allow himself sufficient distance from his offspring.

Steve leans in, and Dad and I follow suit, forming a little huddle. "I've been looking online at similar situations – cancer combined with a serious stroke – and I think palliative care might be our best option."

"What's palliative care?" I ask.

Dad shakes his head. "Steve, I don't think…"

"What?" I ask again. "What is it?"

"Basically hospice," Dad says.

Intense shock rolls up my spine at the word *hospice*. I know that word and what it means… It means giving up. It means comfort. It means *the end.*

"No, not exactly," Steve continues. "Hospice is about making the patient as comfortable as possible. Palliative care is about making the patient comfortable while *still seeking* a cure."

My anxiety eases. "Oh, well, that sounds good then, right? That means Mom won't be in pain, and they aren't giving up on her treatments."

"Exactly," Steve says.

We look at Dad, but he remains silent.

"What are you thinking, Dad?" Steve asks.

"We have a chemo treatment next Monday," he says, sighing. "Yeah," he says after a long minute. "Let's do that."

The door opens, ad I'm surprised at the large array of people entering. I was under the impression that this would be a small meeting between our family and Mom's primary nurse and oncologist, but apparently, I was mistaken. The wide-ranging group of people take up all the remaining seats.

"I'll start things off," the social worker begins. She is probably in her late sixties, and she has short, cropped hair. Like most good social workers, she displays a demeanor that is completely positive. Her eyes probe with compassion into whomever she encounters. "I'll introduce myself, and then we'll just follow in a line. My name is Betsy Hiber, and I am a social worker here at the hospital."

"My name is Devin Strott, and I am a chaplain here."

"You know me. I am Dr. Logan, Annie's oncologist."

"I'm Brittany, Annie's primary nurse."

"And my name is Brody Gibbons. I am another doctor here at the hospital, and I am familiar with your mother's case," the last one says, for some reason, looking at me directly.

"Would you like to continue?" Betsy asks me.

"Oh, sorry," I mutter. "I'm, uh, my name is Emma. I'm her daughter."

"My name is Steve, and I'm Annie's son."

"Jim Morris. Husband."

"Great," Betsy says, nodding. "Well, we're all here to discuss the current situation, as well as your options. I'll let Dr. Gibbons do most of the talking now, at least initially."

"Right," Dr. Gibbon says. "I've been looking at Annie's file this afternoon, and I see that there were some discussions about a release today?"

"That's right," Dad says.

"As I'm sure you're aware, things have drastically changed since this morning," Dr. Gibbons continues. "Your mother suffered a significant stroke, which has impaired her ability to communicate." He again looks directly at me and speaks, which I find unnerving. I wish he would speak directly to Steve, who is clearly the Morris family representative. "I understand that all of you knew the seriousness of Annie's illness, well before today. With the advanced stage of her cancer, unfortunately, we know we are past the idea of looking for a cure."

"True, but we just wanted to prolong *this* as long as we could," Steve says. "Have her live at home for as long as possible."

The young doctor nods. I am sure he is more than qualified to have his job, but he is, without a doubt, the youngest staff member in the room, and I cannot help but find it odd that he is doing all of the talking. He may even be younger than me. I suppose that doesn't say much, except that I have apparently wasted most of my life on meaningless relationships, jobs, and education. No biggie.

"And I think we have finally gotten to that point today," Dr. Gibbons tags on.

My heart stops. I look around the room, with all of the solemn faces seemingly staring down at our small, yet still dwindling, family.

I thought we were discussing options?

A second the length of an hour passes.

This is it, isn't it?

Dr. Logan takes a turn. "This latest stroke, combined with Annie's advanced cancer, has limited our options, unfortunately."

"I've got to get her home," Dad says. His voice surprises me. I haven't heard him act as an advocate for her in the past twelve months as much as I have today. "She has told me all along, for more than a year, that the one thing she didn't want to do was to die in a hospital."

"And that's still an option," Dr. Logan says. "As we see it, there are three *real* options that your family can discuss and choose from. The first is to keep her in this wing of the hospital, in the same room, and monitor her as we have been."

"Absolutely not," Dad says. "We've got to get her out of that room."

Dr. Logan nods empathetically. Even though Dad is being a tad gruff, the entire hospital staff remains completely professional. Who knows how often this particular group gathers together like this... Monthly? Weekly? Daily?

"The second option is to set up a palliative 'slash' hospice care unit at your home," Dr. Logan continues.

Another shock runs through my spine. That word again. *I thought we weren't there yet?*

"I thought palliative care was different from hospice?" Steve asks.

"It is, yes," the doctor says. "Just like you all, we don't want to give up on Annie yet. We want to exhaust all options. 'Palliative' and 'hospice' are just two words that describe the units of care that your mom will need, but we won't shift to 'hospice' care until needed."

"Okay," Steve replies, not exactly convinced.

"We would have nearby nurses, ones within our network and within your insurance network, who would come and care for Annie whenever needed. We would set up specific times for her during the week as well. The nurses, however, would not be present 24/7 at your home."

I scowl, and I notice Steve does the same.

"And the third option is to set her up in our palliative and hospice house, here at the hospital," the doctor concludes. "Have any of you been down there, on the first floor?"

We all shake our heads.

"At the hospice house, we try to make things feel as much like 'home' as we possibly can, but you also have the benefit of 24/7 care provided by a staff of nurses and doctors," Dr. Gibbons says. "You can bring whatever personal items you want to make the space feel more like 'home,' and you can stay however late you want." He pauses and then corrects himself. "Well, the rules have changed slightly as a result of the pandemic, but one of you is allowed to stay in the room all night, if you wish. Up to three people," he says, gesturing to what is left of the Morris family, "can be in the room at the same time. Of course, if things worsen, the rules can be bent slightly so that more of you can be in the room if something were to occur overnight."

"Visiting hours are also open 24/7," Betsy adds. "You just have to sign in and out after each visit."

The entire staff then looks at the three of us, as if we are supposed to have an immediate answer regarding Mom's life.

"So, what'll it be, Morrises? Feel free to take a couple of seconds to decide!"

"This is a big decision," Brittany says, apparently able to read my mind, "so we know you may need some time."

"That's right," Betsy nods. She holds up a finger. "Just know one thing – there is no *wrong* decision here. Whatever decision you will make will be in the best interest of Annie, but they're all *good* decisions."

"Do you have any other questions at the moment?" Dr. Gibbons asks.

The three of us briefly look at each other. We are dazed. We shake our heads limply.

"If you do, we are here to help," the chaplain says. "And I can pray with you over the phone or in person, if you'd like."

He was looking at Dad as he spoke, but it is Steve who answers. "Thank you," he says.

"We'll give you some time now to think things over," Betsy says, "unless you think you know your answer now."

"If you know your answer within the next three seconds, you will receive... a new walker! This luxury item, courtesy of the hospital's overstock inventory, is made of the

finest aluminum metal and will make your experience of navigating your house, which is becoming less and less easy to maneuver in because of the surmounting necessary medical equipment, feel like a joy!"

Dad is the one to break the silence in the confining room this time. "Hospital room is out. I know that." Steve and I both nod in agreement. "So, I guess the option is to set up the care unit at home or here."

Steve and I look at each other. Without saying anything, I know that we are both uncomfortable with Dad being her sole caregiver. Sure, nurses will pop in here and there and whenever needed, but they'll never be there 24/7.

But Mom's only request...

"Your mother did not want to die in a hospital," Dad says loud enough for everyone to hear. The memory of her saying those words has been fresh in my mind all day. "That being said," Dad continues, "I think we could make this as much like home as we possibly could."

"With the 'hospice house,' you mean?" Steve asks. Dad nods. "What do you think, Em?"

I feel hotness rise in my face as I am put on the spot. Mom's life is not solely in my hands, but I suddenly feel as though it is. "I think," I stammer, "that's our only viable option."

"So, you're all in agreement?" Dr. Gibbons asks.

We all reply "yes" clumsily.

"Okay, we'll get to work on that then," Dr. Gibbons says, standing up.

"Given the situation, you made a good choice," Betsy says as the rest of the group comes around to shake our hands and say goodbye.

The chaplain is the last to leave. He once again offers his services to Dad. "Sometimes situations like these require more than just the medical professionals," he says. "Please, don't forget about me." He hands Dad his card and leaves.

The loud clock of the door is the only sound for a solid minute. There is no Judge Judy to disrupt the moment this time. The three of us must each internally face the huge moment before us and handle it in our own way.

"Do you think she was right?" Steve asks. "That social worker?"

"I do," I answer. "I think this is the right choice."

"Dad?" Steve asks.

As he stands, Dad groans, and I can hear clicks and pops snap rapidly within his joints. His old, aching body sounds like a car engine trying to start too quickly on a morning that is ten degrees below zero.

"Let's go get your mother's things."

PART TWO

A New Home

6

"Who are you hear to see?"

"Annie Morris."

The door buzzes open.

Dad, Steve, and I enter the hospice house of the hospital. It is located on the first floor near one of the main entrances, and, frankly, I'm surprised I have never noticed it before. Perhaps my subconscious was protecting me, knowing my future turmoil.

This particular wing of the hospital is dimly lit, and I cannot help but think the darkness has nothing to do with the late hour. It feels more thematic.

"You'll be going to room 7," the nurse at the front station tells us. "Here are your badges. Make sure you sign in over there at that table." She points to a table across the room. A large notebook sits on top of it, alongside a glass jar of candy. Since they couldn't install a bar to give visitors a chance to take a shot of liquid courage before seeing their deteriorating loved ones, giving families a minor sugar rush was the next best idea, I guess. "When you're done visiting, just return your badges to either nurse's station, and be sure to sign out in the same book."

"Thanks," Steve says.

After we all sign in, we begin our slow walk down the hall. Earlier, Dad had already transported Mom's belongings from her hospital room on the fifth floor. Even though he'd been down here already, he still walks apprehensively behind us.

We peek in each room as we pass it. The first room on the left is some sort of religious center or prayer room. A podium stands at the front of the room, with rows of chairs before it. Lining line both sides of the room, bookcases are filled with religious books from the heavy-hitters you might expect to see on local TV early Sunday morning. And lastly, tucked away high on one of the bookshelves, is a small menorah. *Mazel tov.*

The hallway turns, and as we follow it, I see a small lobby to the left, complete with a sofa, two large chairs, a love seat, and another bookcase. This one is filled with the usual fictional giants you'd see on any small, gas-station book stand in America – Tom Clancy, Danielle Steele, Clive Cussler, Dean Koontz, Nora Roberts, and Louis L'Amour. I don't know why I pay so much attention to the books on any of the shelves. Reading, or enjoying anything for that matter, does not interest me in the slightest at the moment.

The onslaught of patient rooms follows. They line both sides of the hallway. Although I don't "intend" to, as I pass, I look into every room with an open door. Sometimes the room is empty; sometimes there is a family member sitting at the foot of a bed, staring back at me; and sometimes there is only a patient, staring up towards the ceiling.

Finally, we reach room 7, and I realize just how unprepared I am for the moment. I try, and fail, to take a subtle deep breath as Dad places his hand on the door. He looks back at us and asks, "You ready?"

Steve and I both nod. The wide, barn-sized door creaks open.

Mom.

The room is dark and not terribly big, but it is undeniably better than the hospital rooms upstairs. Although the "family meeting" group told us we could make this as much like home as we wanted, I begin to fear the possibility of that.

Look at her.

To the left of her bed is a recliner that, somehow, is able to fold out into a bed. Another small recliner sits opposite it, complete with a matching footstool. And then to the right of the bed is a more typical sitting chair. Nothing fancy. Three seats for a maximum of three visitors, in other words.

Don't be afraid. Just look at her.

A small TV hangs on the wall in front of her bed. A sink sits underneath, and next to the sink is a bathroom. Nothing else major complements the room.

She's your mom.

I take a breath. I know I need to face reality and stop focusing on the small things, like Sherlock Holmes does by making mental notes. I need to recognize the reason I am here.

This wasn't supposed to happen.
Not yet.
Not today.

I look at her.

She is breathing softly. A blanket covers most of her body, which I know she would hate. Her body temperature was always about fifteen degrees higher than everyone else's. She always blamed the great change in her body's chemistry on my birth – her second and final – in particular. I was never sure what I was supposed to take away from her claim or how I should feel about it, but I always did feel some sort of weird guilt. It kinda explains my mental instability when I think about it now – I was born in a way that caused discomfort (beyond the usual discomfort caused by labor) to my mom. Therefore, I will forever be haunted by the same curse, like some sort of anxiety werewolf.

"Hey, Mom," I say as I approach the bed and pull down the blanket a bit. "It's Emma. Steve and Dad are here, too."

Mom groans and slightly turns her head. It appears as though she is squinting to try to see if her family is truly beside her or if it is her delirium getting worse.

"Hey, Mom," Steve says stepping forward. Dad moves to the other side of the bed. He places his hand on hers. I know I shouldn't be bothered by him in this moment, but I still am.

Mom shifts her head again with great effort. She looks so much worse than she did just a few hours ago, when we fed her a piece of birthday cake. I have never been so aware of how vulnerable a person's mortality is than in this moment.

"Don't make yourself uncomfortable, Hun," Dad says. "We'll be right here with you."

I scoff. *How could he possibly lie to her face like that? And right now?*

I feel a nudge in my arm. I look over my shoulder. Steve is giving me a "just chill out" face. I roll my eyes.

"Hello," a nurse says from behind us. His voice is low and calm. "My name is Geoffrey, and I'll be Annie's nurse tonight. I know you just got down here and that it's been a busy day for you all. We were going to go ahead and give her a bath now, if that's okay? We like to take care of those things as soon as the new nursing shift begins, which it just did."

Dad stands with the usual level of agony. "Oh, sure. We'll get out of your hair."

"So you're here all night?" Steve asks Geoffrey.

"That's right, and I'll actually be stationed right outside this room."

I finally catch a breath. "That's a relief."

"Absolutely. I'll be monitoring her all night, and I'll be in touch with all of you if something were to happen." Geoffrey looks down at his chart. "We like to keep two main phone numbers on file. I believe I have your number," he says, pointing to Dad, "and yours," he says pointing to Steve. He looks to me next. "Do you want me to write yours down as well?"

"I'm staying with my brother for the time being, so you can just get ahold of Steve."

"Perfect."

I already like Geoffrey, but I *despise* how everyone constantly says "perfect" now. What's perfect? Nothing is perfect. Certainly nothing about this situation.

"We'll get started on that as soon as all of you are ready," Geoffrey says as he leaves the room.

"I like him," Steve says. I nod in agreement. Dad remains still. "You're in good hands, Mom," Steve continues. "We'll be back in just a little bit."

And just like that, less than ten minutes after seeing Mom, in what inevitably will be her death bed, we are booted from the room. Tensions are high. We can all feel it.

It is only a matter of time before one of us explodes.

7

Steve and I sit together on the sofa in the lobby of the hospice house, and Dad finds a recliner nearby. We sit in silence for a moment, and then Dad cranes his neck to look at the bookshelf.

Ugh, why do I have to be like him at all?

"Well, ain't that thing just loaded up with the worst literature of the Twentieth Century?" he scoffs.

Steve looks over and looks away just as quickly, disinterested. "Probably stuff left behind by families of patients."

"Yeah, I doubt they go out hunting for great book deals," I add.

Dad starts to pick at his teeth with a toothpick produced from God-knows-where. It's one of his habits I hate most. "Still. Just shows you how stupid the population is."

"Well, what should they be reading, Dad?" Steve asks, surprisingly annoyed. It usually takes him much longer than me to reach his wit's end, but this has been a hell of a day for us all. "The book you wrote about independent filmmaking?"

Ouch. Nice one, Brother.

Dad glares at him. "Sold more than a few copies of that, thank you very much. But no, Smartass, not my book. Something more, you know... *profound*. Thematically deep."

I know where he's going with this, and I want to avoid the conversation at all costs. Steve, however, is apparently more willing to fall into Dad's trap.

"Well, like what?" Steve asks again, annoyed. "Hemingway? Faulkner?"

"Well, sure, but you know I don't go much for fiction... Except Hemingway, of course. But *The Green Hills of Africa* is better than *A Farewell to Arms*... with all that *romance*. Give me big game hunting adventures any day of the week."

Please...

"I think the best books are non-fiction..."

Stop...

"Like the works of..."

"William F. Buckley, Jr.," Dad and I say together.

He looks over at me, somehow surprised that I would guess who his favorite author is, even though I think he is the only author he's actually read at-length. "Yeah, we know," I finish.

"Well, what the hell's wrong with a great American like William F. Buckley, Jr.?" he asks me.

"Technically, nothing – as long as he's not the *only* author you read," I reply.

"He's not the only author I read. Didn't you just hear me talk about Hemingway?"

"As far as political, non-fiction authors go, you run his fan club."

"I've read plenty of other political..."

"The speeches of Barry Goldwater don't count."

He glares at me. "You got a problem, Little Lady?"

"Em, don't," Steve whispers to me. He's a coward, though. He slouches down so Dad cannot see him talking to me.

"Yeah, I think I do," I answer. "I've listened – *silently*, mind you – to you ramble on and on about your neoconservative political beliefs my entire life, and I just don't think I can take anymore. Especially not today."

Dad perches himself up in his seat. He is getting into his fighting position.

"Oh, no," Steve moans under his breath. "Why, Em?"

"Shut up, Steve!" I shout. "Don't act like you don't say the exact same things as me as soon as he leaves the room."

Dad looks at him, and Steve's eyes shift quickly, not knowing what to do or which side to take – or rather, which side will result in a lesser casualty to himself. "I am not a neocon," Dad enunciates slowly. "I am an independent."

I roll my eyes. "Again with this crap?"

He points a finger at me. "You better watch yourself."

"Or what?" I scoff. "You'll ground me? I'm thirty-two years old!"

"Your generation…" he growls. "You'll never know what it means to work hard or what it feels like to actually sacrifice something from yourself."

"'My generation' nothing!" I return. "All we've done our entire lives is clean up after your generation's mess! Wars, climate, economic instability… And don't get me started on 'sacrifice.' You really don't want to go there, Dad…"

Steve suddenly breaks in. "Guys. Can we quiet down, please? We don't need to be having a political debate right now, and we certainly don't need to be shouting *in the hospice lobby!*" He ironically whisper-shouts the last four words.

I slowly lean back into the couch. Sensing a cease-fire, Dad eases out of his fighting stance as well.

"Thank you," Steve says. "Now let's figure out the situation at hand tonight."

"What do you mean?" I ask.

"Only one of us can stay," he reminds us. "I am open to all suggestions, but I'll be more than happy to stay with Mom. Em, you have a key to my house, so you can get in without me."

"What about clothes and stuff?" I ask.

"I'll be fine overnight. I can go change in the morning when one of you gets here." He stops talking and looks at Dad. "Well, what do think?"

"Yeah, that might be all right," Dad answers. "I can go home tonight, get some stuff, sleep a bit, and be ready for a full day tomorrow."

I cannot help but feel hurt on behalf of Mom. Sure, Steve and I both *want* to be with Mom, but Dad shouldn't have even let us entertain a discussion about it. He should have *insisted* on his staying. I bury my anger deep, however, and withhold from saying anything.

"Okay, we'll do that then," Steve says. He really is the glue of our family. God help us if he is the next to go. Dad and I would never see each other again.

I stand and glance down the hallway. There is no movement. "How much longer do you think her bath will take?"

"Not sure," Steve says. "Usually takes 'em a half an hour, or at least it did upstairs. Probably be longer now that…" Steve does not finish his thought, but he doesn't need to.

"Wish there was a TV in here," Dad grumbles.

I do a slow turn. "I'm sure that *minor* detail got overlooked when they were decorating the *hospice house*."

"Just saying. I like the noise."

I feel anger boil within me again. I try to hold it in, but I know that its outpouring is inevitable. "Why is TV so damned important to you?"

"It gave me a *career* for one, Em," he says in a "duh" voice. He does not say anything else, but I could tell by the way he said "career" that he was being demeaning toward me. He is well aware that I have had nothing of a career in my life. I've held one pointless job after another, none ever lasting more than a year.

"Was that why you were on the phone all morning?" I shoot back. "You know, while Mom was having a stroke?"

Dad's eyes burn into me and I am, legitimately, scared. He has never looked so angrily at me before in my life. I know I have crossed a line.

Steve picks up on the dire situation instantly. "Emma, that's enough." He does not hide when he speaks this time. He has firmly chosen a side for this side argument.

"You're right," I say softly. "I apologize." I lean back into the couch, like a whipped dog, tail between my legs. I am no longer looking at him, but I know Dad is still shooting lasers at me.

Then, abruptly, Dad stands up. "I'm gonna head out. Got an hour drive ahead of me. I'll be back early." He walks away and never once looks at us.

"What was that?" Steve demands as soon as Dad is out of earshot.

Suddenly, my anger returns and is now directed at a new target. "I didn't say anything untrue. I'm glad he feels guilty. I wish I hadn't apologized."

Steve shakes his head. "How are we going to get through this?" he says to himself.

8

The next morning, I arrive at the hospital a little after eight o'clock. I had gotten back to Steve's place at around midnight, and I went straight to bed. I stared at the ceiling for a good hour, never once feeling tired. I didn't even turn on music or a podcast, which I do every single night. I just stared off into the darkness in complete silence. I don't even remember what I thought about. I think my brain was just so overloaded from the day before – a day that felt like a year.

Eventually, by some miracle, I was able to fall asleep. I slept in Lucas's twin-sized bed, complete with dinosaur bedding. I'm not ashamed to admit that I did indeed snuggle with a triceratops last night.

Lucas is Steve's three-year-old son, but he only stays with his father one weekend out of the month. Steve is a great father – person, in general – so I found the custody arrangement particularly stern. I guess it is just hard for a dad, no matter how great he is, to get to see his kid for an equal amount of time when the mom is a functional adult with no major issues. *Major* issues.

When I awoke, I was disappointed in myself. I don't know when I expected to get to the hospital the next morning, but I still felt as though it should have been earlier. So as soon as I was fully awake, I tossed aside Ezekiel (I named the triceratops), and quickly got ready. I grabbed yesterday's jeans and a new shirt and threw my hair into a messy bun. I rolled on some deodorant while I brushed my teeth (I still don't know how I managed to do that one – it was kind of like a pat your head, rub your tummy sort of routine), and then I grabbed a cup of coffee – that Steve had graciously left behind the morning before – and threw it in the microwave for two minutes. While the tray spun, I threw on my Vans and gave myself a quick once over. Not being overly horrified, I was out the door by the time the microwave finished beeping.

Steve was already up and looking fresh by the time I got to Mom's room. In fact, he had already converted his bed back into a recliner. I was a tad disappointed – I wanted to see just how that worked. He was sitting in it and talking to Mom when I opened the door.

"Oh, sorry," I say as soon as I see him.

"No, you're fine," he says, waving me off. "I've already gotten to talk to her a lot this morning." My heart breaks when he says that. He gives me one of those "yeah, I know" smirks. "Do you want some time with her?"

I take a shallow breath. "No that's okay, I think…" I stop. *Why am I always doing that? Denying what I want?* "Actually, yeah," I correct myself, "I think I do. I don't need long."

"Take your time. I'll be in the lobby when you're finished," he says as he leaves the room.

I look down at my mom. She looks about the same as she did yesterday, but I know she is not. Each day is just one day closer.

"Hey, Mom. Sorry I got here so late. I slept in Lucas's bed last night. I'd blame my lateness on that, but I actually slept all right... given the circumstances."

I pause, not knowing what to say next. Mom continues to breathe at the same slow rate. She is looking off into the distance. It does not look as though she is listening to me, but I know she is.

One day closer.

I need to *really* come to terms with that. I can no longer avoid saying certain things because I may be uncomfortable. *She* is the one who is uncomfortable. What she needs, more than anything else right now, is just... us.

I shift on my feet as I stand beside her bed. "I'm sorry. I don't know where to even begin. I've never had to have a conversation like this before."

I look down and spot Mom's hand, specifically her index finger and thumb. They move slightly, forming a "pinching" movement. I let out one loud laugh that immediately turns into a cry. I grab the nearest chair and sit down. I sob into my hands.

It may look like nothing, but she is making a calculated movement. When Steve and I were little – like, *really* little – Mom used to torture us with this thing called a "tickle bug." She would pinch those two fingers together, when we were least expecting it, and announce that the tickle bug was back. Steve and I would shoot up from our seats as she playfully chased us around. If the bug got us, we would suffer a swarm of unrelenting tickles on our sides.

I raise my head and grin ear-to-ear. "The tickle bug's gonna get me?" I laugh.

A small smirk appears on Mom's face. Then her hand suddenly stops and does a new movement – all five fingers move in a slow, rolling motion.

This I expected. Step two in our "tickle torture" sessions involved the arrival of an arachnid – specifically, the "tickle spider." Once the tickle bug had met its satisfaction, his close relative would quickly arrive and chase us around just as soon as Steve and I had caught our breath.

The tickle spider was more intense in its attack. While the bug focused its tickles primarily on our ribs, the spider could latch on anywhere. He was also much stronger than the bug and could hang on through our intense flailing. Also, like most spiders, the tickle spider was rarely alone. He often traveled with his twin sidekick, who only appeared after the first spider was firmly latched on to one of us.

"And now the tickle spider?" I laugh again. "I'm in a serious amount of danger."

Mom's hand drops, and I place mine over hers. She still looks off into the distance, but it is so comforting to know she is still with me. I no longer feel guarded with my words.

"I'm sorry I didn't say 'I love you' more. I mean, I know I said it to you plenty of times, and you know I've always loved you, but I'm sorry I didn't *actually* say it more. The words. Especially in high school. I was kind of a mess then. I guess I still am in ways, but whatever. This isn't about me.

"Do you remember that one time we had that huge fight? I was in college, and I was home for the weekend. I'm sure you remember. It was one of those all-out screaming matches. I was so pissed off at Jake – sorry, I know I shouldn't say 'piss'... sorry, again. Anyway, I said some things to you that day that I shouldn't have. I never should have spoken to you like that. Ever. I've felt so bad about that for years now. I don't know why I didn't say something sooner. Even when you're an adult, I guess it's hard to apologize to a parent. Our stubbornness from being a kid is just so hard to shake off.

"I also wish I had made more time for just the two of us, ya know? We spent a lot of time together when we were growing up, especially while Dad was out of town working, but we should have – I mean, *I* should have – made more of an effort to do that as I got older, too.

"I wish I hadn't waited until your cancer diagnosis to ask you more personal questions. You know, about your life before Dad and all of that. But even the 'Dad years,' too, before Steve and I came along. I loved talking about that stuff with you during this past year.

"I wasted a lot of time."

I begin to cry again, feeling the weight of disappointment in myself. As I try to regain control of my stuffy nose, I hear the curtain move behind me. I quickly wipe my eyes.

"I'm so sorry, Emma," Geoffrey says. "I can give you another minute."

"No, that's okay. You remembered my name?" I say with a chuckle, sniffling.

Geoffrey looks confused. "Of course, I do. I'm your mom's nurse. You are important to her."

I cry again. I see the look of worry on Geoffrey's face, and I quickly wave it off. "You're fine. It's just... hard."

"I know it is."

"I don't know how you could do this job."

He smiles. "My father died when I was in high school. He was all I had growing up. No siblings, no mother. Like your mom, he was diagnosed with cancer, and like you, I sat with him every day he was in hospice."

My eyes widen. "This seems like this is the last place you'd want to be then."

"Quite the opposite. When I'm working in this wing of the hospital, I feel like… this is the closest I can be to him. I know it sounds crazy, but we all get to a point in our lives where nothing really makes sense anymore. For me, that was in high school when he died."

"I'm so sorry."

His face lights up. "It's okay. Really. I love my job. I like feeling as though I'm still connected to my dad." He then looks at me directly. "But mostly I like feeling as though I can help others feel better through this terrible process. Because I know what it feels like, and I know what I would have wanted and needed when I was down here, alone, with him every day until the end."

I have rarely felt gratitude like I feel for Geoffrey in this moment. "Thank you," I say simply.

"It's my job," he says, brushing me off, "but you're welcome."

Steve sticks his head in the room. "Just wanted to make sure everything was okay. I saw you come in and…"

"Everything is fine. I just wanted to come by and check the usual things – blood pressure, oxygen, movement…"

"Oh okay, sounds good," Steve says and then beckons me with a movement of his head. I follow him out of the room.

"What's up?" I ask him as we walk down the hallway toward the lobby.

"Nothing, I just…"

"What?"

"Well, Mallory called me this morning."

I cringe every time I hear the name of his ex-wife. I don't like that she cheated on him, I don't like that she has the majority of their kid's custody, and I don't like that *she* was the one who filed the divorce against *him*. Selfishly, I also don't like the fact that I lost, probably, my best friend in the process. Mallory and I were inseparable for the four years they were together. We probably spent more nights together than she and Steve did.

Maybe even more nights than she shared with that douchebag, Derrick.

"Hello?"

"Sorry, Steve. My brain's just kinda…" I make some whacky motion with my hand. "So what did *Mallory* want?"

Steve doesn't feed into my antics. "She offered to let Lucas come visit me today."

"Oh, how generous of her."

"That's not what I'm getting at."

"What are you getting at then?"

He thinks it over. "Do I let him say goodbye to his grandma?"

Ouch. My chest hurts for Lucas, Steve, and myself all at once. "I mean, that's your decision…"

"I just don't know what to do. She watched him for two and a half years while I worked... went through a divorce... They became best friends." His head drops. "I just don't know if I should let the 'old' version of her remain the version that he'll probably remember." Steve traces the outline of a tile with his shoe. "Or what if she's holding out to see him? Or anyone, for that matter? I just don't know."

Steve plops down onto the sofa where we sat last night. I gently follow suit. "I think you should do what you think is best." I then swallow my pride for what I am about to say. "I think you should consult... Mallory and see what she thinks too."

"What would you do if he were your son?"

This is some heavy stuff.

"Why don't you talk to Lucas about it?"

Steve looks at me. The thought clearly had not occurred to him. "Thanks, Em."

9

At 10:08 a.m., Dad finally makes an appearance.

"Hey, Kiddos," he says, looking only at Steve, "what's the word?"

"Nothing much has changed," Steve replies.

Dad takes the remaining seat at the foot of Mom's bed. "She do okay overnight?"

"She did okay. There were a few times where I could tell she was definitely uncomfortable... moaned a bit. I told Geoffrey about it, though, and he came right in, fixed her up."

"He's the uh..."

"The *nurse*," I assert. "That's right."

Don't you dare say anything demeaning about Geoffrey. I'll cut you.

Dad places a hand on Mom's foot. "Hey, Hun. Sorry I was late this morning."

"Lotta calls to make?" I ask.

Dad keeps his eyes on Mom, but his lip curls as he grinds his teeth.

"Why don't we give Dad a minute with her?" Steve suggests. "We both had some time with her this morning."

Steve stands and nearly pulls me out of my chair.

When we reach the lobby, Steve starts in on me, as I predicted. "Not in there!" he whispers. "Do that shit out here if you must, although I'd rather you not do it at all. But not in there. Not in front of Mom."

I fight back my intense need to physically throw down with him. No one points a finger at me and tells me what to do. Not even my brother. "It's after *ten o'clock*..."

"I don't care, Em. I really don't. We cannot control his actions. We never could. That should be painfully obvious to us by now. We can only control ourselves and how *we* want Mom's final days to be."

As pissed off as I am, I know he is right. "Fine."

"I seriously don't get you," he continues on. "Why would you want to provoke and create a fight like that in front of her?"

"I. Said. 'FINE.'"

Steve's tensions ease up. "Okay. Sorry for yelling."

"And for telling me what to do?"

"And for telling you what to do."

"And for pointing your finger at me?"

Steve laughs. "All right! I'm sorry."

We both look over at the lobby bookshelf. "You make a decision about Lucas yet?" I ask.

"Mallory's bringing him by at noon. Gonna meet them outside. I'll talk to him then."

"What if he says no? Or, you know, doesn't really *get it*?"

He sighs. "I don't know." He runs his fingers through his hair, overwhelmed. "I don't know."

I feel bad for Lucas and him, I really do. Steve and I aren't really the "hugging" type of siblings, so he looks alarmed when I place a hand on his shoulder. "Whatever decision you make will be the right one."

Steve smiles. "Thanks."

I give him a couple of sturdy pats and then drop my hand.

Steve then looks back up at me, confused. "Did you just quote Betsy? The social worker?"

"No." I act offended.

"I think you did."

My brow furrows. "Subconsciously… yeah, I think I did."

"Don't do that ever again," he laughs.

I laugh with him. It's so nice to have a sibling who understands me the way Steve does. He would never admit it, but he would say the same about me.

Something then catches my eye on the bookshelf. "That son of a bitch."

"What?" Steve asks, shocked.

I point to the spine of one of the books. "You see this shit?"

Steve turns his head sideways. "William F. Buckley, Jr.? You don't think…?"

"That Dad planted that on the shelf before he came into Mom's room this morning? Yeah, I do."

Steve chuckles. "You gotta give it to him – he's one of a kind."

10

"Mom, I want to show you something."

She moans lightly in response to Steve's voice. I'm in the room too while Dad is in the hallway restroom. He was going to use the one in her room, but when I heard the rumbles in his stomach, I demanded he take it elsewhere. We're dealing with enough in here.

Steve leans closer in and holds up his phone to her, showing her a video from his Snapchat. He chuckles as he starts the video. "Hey, Grandma!"

I had been scrolling through endless, pointless social media posts on my own phone, but I stop when I hear my nephew's voice.

"Gramma still at the hospital?" Lucas asks in the video.

Off-camera, Mallory says, "That's right, Buddy. She is. What do you want to say to her?"

"I miss you, Gramma. Wanna watch 'Patrapol' with me?"

I frown as I watch him play the video, but Steve is all smiles. "Hear that, Mom? Lucas said he wants to watch *Paw Patrol* with you." He closes the app on his phone. "You created a monster with that boy. All he wants to do is watch that show now. Specifically, he wants to watch it with you before naptime."

Mom mumbles something, and we both lean closer. It's the closest thing to audible words we have heard from her since before her big stroke.

"What? What did you say?" Steve asks.

Mom's lips open and shut slightly as she clearly attempts to form words. "Tlemcmplyhrr." There are words in there, but it's still just a mumble to us.

"Sorry, Mom, try saying it again."

"Telhmtocmplyherr."

"I think she said…" I start.

"Tell him to come play here," Steve finishes. He looks over at me, devastated. He then turns back to Mom and brushes her hair with his hand. "I wish he could play here," he says, holding back tears. "We don't have any toys here. But I'll try and see if I can get him to come here."

Steve stands. "Hey…" I begin, but he walks out. He brushes by Dad as he re-enters.

"What's the matter?" he asks. "You look kinda… shaken."

"Mom just… kinda talked," I reply, dumb-founded.

Dad sits down with a plop. "She did? What did she say?"

"Steve was playing her a video of Lucas, and she told him to 'come play here.'"

Dad eyes grow distant. "She really said that?"

It's the first time, in months, that I have felt any sort of kinship with him. It sounds hyperbolic, but it's also the first time, in months, that I have felt like he has grasped the severity of the situation.

"Hey, Em?" Dad says to me after a moment. His eyes remain on his wife. "Could you give me a minute with your mom?" He looks over at me. The eyes full of hatred that I saw last night are completely gone. The eyes I see now are the ones I knew growing up.

He's back.

"Yeah, sure. I'll go check on Steve."

"Hey, Brother."

Steve's eyes remain focused on the floor. "I can't take Lucas in there, Em."

I sit down next to him on the couch. I do not really want to offer my input – it's not really my place to say what he should or should not do with his son. "You don't have to make a rash decision."

He looks up at the clock. "I kinda do." He sighs, "Do you remember when Papa died?"

"Yeah," I answer solemnly. "Well, barely."

"That's my point. You were, what, five years old when he died? I was almost ten. I remember things about that night – getting told he had a heart attack, going up to console Grandma, and then getting things ready for his funeral those next few days. But what I really remember most is him lying there – in that coffin. I used to have nightmares about it. I'd dream that he would slowly rise up, like Dracula, and then step out of it with his long legs. Then he'd come after me. Not in a mean way, but it was still scary. Having those nightmares caused me to sleepwalk for, like, a year."

"I remember."

"Do you remember Papa in his coffin?"

"No," I answer. "I just remember Mom being sad that he was gone." I think back. "Oddly enough, I remember her picking out clothes from his dresser to prepare him for the funeral."

"Lucas is younger than either of us were, so what's the best we could expect if I took him back there? He'd either never remember it, or worse, he might be scarred from it – seeing Grandma like he never has before." Steve shakes his head as tears start to come. "But she asked for him. How can I say no?"

I wish I had an answer for him, but the truth is I don't. I do not know what Steve should do. All of his points are valid. In my attempt to come to some sort of solution for him, I end up just remaining quiet.

Steve stands, with a groan of great emotional weight. "I gotta go outside and meet them."

"What are you gonna do?" I ask simply.

"I'll let you know when I know."

As Steve walks away, I am left alone in the lobby. I cannot help but think how our close-knit, "nuclear" family has now become a bunch of loners. I'm alone without a husband, boyfriend, children, or even a dog. Steve is alone most weeks, without his son and ex-wife. Dad is soon to be alone, losing Mom. And Mom… well, she probably feels the most alone out of all of us right now. Alone in her situation, her pain, her understanding of what it means to be at the end of one's life… alone in her knowledge of what it feels like to be the first one to leave a loving family.

As I weigh the heaviness of the eternal, I can only hope that Dad is making amends with her, right now, in that room.

11

As I look through Amazon marketplace, trying to find *good* books to place in this hospice library, as well as trying to get my mind off the most depressing day of my life so far, I see Dad emerge in my periphery.

"Em…" he says, shaking his head.

"What?" I ask with a shot. I immediately stand up, sensing the worst.

"She's not responding anymore."

"What do you mean 'not responding'?"

"She's not even attempting to formulate words anymore. She's no longer gesturing with her hands or head. She's just…"

"When did this happen? Just now? Did you call in Geoffrey?"

"Yes and yes. A couple of nurses are in there now."

"Are we going to run tests or…?"

"Em," he says again softly. "The time for testing is over. Look at where we are."

"So, we're just giving up? We're not gonna try anything? For her sake?"

"This is hospice. This is not a recovery center. These things are going to happen. More and more, until…" he stops.

I try to comprehend this new devastating news. "Mom's never going to talk to me again?" I pause again. "I'm never going to hear her voice again?"

I never realized before this moment how important a person's voice is. We take something so seemingly minute like that for granted, and yet there is nothing more powerful than a person's voice. It is defining. It captures a person's soul. I search my brain trying to remember if we had ever recorded her voice. I become frightened, knowing that we never had. *How could we have been so stupid? Now it's too late...*

Dad sits down with a thud in one of the chairs across the room. He stares off into the distance.

I begin to shake my head, getting angry. "Why didn't you call me in?" I yell. "Steve and I were both right here, fifty feet away!"

"It's not like I had a warning, Em. It just happened."

"Were you talking to her?"

"Of course, I was."

"What did you say?"

He looks over at me slowly. "I don't need to tell you everything. You're still my daughter."

"You didn't deserve her last words!" I shout. I know I am being too loud, and the last thing I want to do is scare any of the patients or get kicked out of the hospice house, but my anger has been swelling inside me and now it consumes me.

Dad leans forward in his chair, looking up at me. "She's my wife. I have been with her..."

"You didn't treat her like your wife, your loved one, or your partner. You just ran off to do your next job at every opportunity, leaving all of us without any consideration."

Bringing up Dad's absenteeism is a sure-fire way to anger him, and that is exactly what I have done. He stands up, like a bear about to attack. He speaks through clenched teeth. "I did not leave you 'without any consideration.' I had a job to do."

"*Jobs*," I emphasize. "You could never take a break between them or, God forbid, turn one down. You did anything to get out of our house – to leave Mom."

Although I previously thought it was unlikely, I detect that Dad is about to hit me. Sensing the incoming pain, but certainly unwilling to turn away or back down from him, I close my eyes and tense up, ready to take his worst.

"What are you two doing?" Steve shouts in a hushed tone.

His words snap us back into reality. Dad and I both look down and see Lucas, who seems terrified – of the hospital, of the low lighting, and of his aunt and grandfather fighting. He grabs Steve's leg and backs himself behind it.

All animosity leaves my body when I see him. "Luke, come over here," I say, crouching down with outstretched arms. Lucas looks up at his dad, who nudges him. He slowly comes over. I sweep him up into a loving hug. "How are you, Turd Bucket?"

"Em," I hear Steve disapprovingly say.

"Sorry," I mutter. I squeeze Lucas even harder and he finally reciprocates. I then hold him out at arm's length. "Are you okay? Is it scary in here?"

Lucas nods.

"Don't worry, we got you. It's not scary in here. It's just a bunch of families hanging out together."

This new information seems to ease Lucas's tensions. He finally speaks. "Where's Gramma?"

I look up at Steve. "I need to talk to you before you do anything," I attempt to whisper.

Steve then crouches down with us. "Hey, I need to talk to Aunt Em for a sec," he tells his son. "Is that okay?"

Lucas shakes his head.

Steve smiles painfully. "I know it's hard. But Grandpa will sit with you," he says, looking over. "Won't you?"

"Of course, I will," he says, ambling over. He parks himself on the couch and pats the seat next to him. "Come here, Kiddo."

Lucas once again looks up at Steve. "Here," he says, reaching into his pocket, "you can have my phone. *For just a minute.* But you can only play your 'pancake' game – no YouTube. Okay?"

Lucas snatches the phone and climbs up next to his grandfather. Dad puts his arm around him and steals a hug, which is the only way he's probably going to get one at the moment.

"I'll be right back, Buster," Steve says.

I update my brother on Mom's current state, and he clearly struggles to absorb it.

"So that's it?" he asks simply.

I nod. "That's it."

He sighs heavily. "Shit."

"What are you going to do with Lucas? Are you going to take him back there?"

It is clear Steve had already made a decision, but current events have altered things once again. "What am I supposed to do? Take him in there, and have Mom not react to him? That'll break his heart."

I rub my imaginary beard. "You could tell him she's asleep?"

Steve looks up, interest piqued.

"That way he can still get closure if he needs it and, even more importantly, if she needs it." I chuckle and add, "Luke knows how much Grandma loves her naps."

"True," Steve says. His mouth moves into a grin, but his eyes remain sad and heavy. "Okay," he finally says. "I think that's a good idea. Thanks, Em."

I watch as Steve goes back to Lucas and lifts him off the couch. Lucas is certainly old enough to navigate the hallway himself, but Steve knows how frightened he is. I smile and wave as they walk toward Mom's room. The closer they get to their destination, the tighter Lucas holds onto his dad, head burrowed into his neck.

12

To my surprise, Lucas comes walking back into the lobby on his own. Dad is still on the couch, while I purposefully sit in the furthest chair away from him. Despite our animosity towards each other, however, we bury the hatchet anytime Lucas is around. Steve follows a couple of steps behind him.

"Gramma was sleeping," Lucas informs us.

"Oh, yeah?" I ask.

"Yeah, and she... she... feels better now. She will feel better after her nap."

I look up at Steve, who is having to fight back tears with all of his might. "That's right, Buster."

"Did you talk to Grandma?" I ask my nephew.

"Yes."

"What did you talk about?"

"I told her I am going to her house soon and that she isn't staying here. She isn't staying here." He comes and sits on my lap.

"No, she won't have to stay here too much longer," I say, hugging him. "She'll feel a lot better soon."

"After her nap."

I smile. "That's right."

"I hugged Gramma."

My eyes swell. "You did?"

"Dad picked me up, and I hugged her. She was sleeping so she didn't hug back, but I did."

"How'd that make you feel?" I ask, worrying if even something small like that could emotionally scar him.

His eyes scan the room. "Good. I like hugging Gramma."

"Me too," I say.

"Dad, can we go balance?"

Most kids like to go to playgrounds, play in water, or find a ball to throw and kick. Not Lucas. He like to find walls made of stone, like the ones found in parking garages, and walk across them. It's his favorite activity. He calls it "balancing."

Steve laughs. "Yeah, we'll go balance. But you've got to hold my hand. Those walls we saw on the way in were kinda tall."

"I don't wanna hold your hand."

"Lucas Matthew…"

I cringe when I hear my father's middle name. I wish Steve had chosen another name for Lucas – any other name.

"Fine," Lucas agrees. "Come on!"

"I'll be back in a few. Mallory's picking him up soon. I'll come back up after that." He glances between us. "Can you two handle yourselves?"

Dad and I both groan.

Once Steve and Lucas are gone, my brief moment of semi-happiness evaporates again as I realize I am once more sharing a room with only my father. I peek across the room. He does not appear to be much more thrilled than I am.

I pull out my phone and begin book shopping again. *Maybe Shakespeare? Like a modern English version of one of his plays. But then again, who actually* wants *to read the Bard, let alone in a hospice house? Something more modern, but still classy. Maybe* Beloved *by Toni Morrison or something by James Baldwin?* Go Tell It on the Mountain *would be good. Oooh,* First Blood *is actually really good – better than the movie. Or maybe a Raymond Chandler? No, he's confusing...*

"Emma?"

I look up from my phone right after I add *The Last Picture Show* by Larry McMurty to my digital shopping cart. "Yeah?" I ask, put upon.

"Why do you think I'm here?"

I look around. "You mean, in this lobby?"

"Why am I here, in this hospital?"

I shake my head. "I honestly don't know."

"You *really* don't think I care about your mother? My wife?"

I exhale loudly. "It's not that I don't think you *care* about her, I just think that... you didn't care *enough*."

He nods, pursing his lips. "Do you know how I met her?"

My eyes roll back, trying to find a memory. "Um, not really. Wasn't it in college?"

"It was the summer after I graduated high school. I was touring a college campus, and you know how they put you in those obnoxious groups to try and ice-break you with your soon-to-be fellow students? Well, she ended up in a group with me. The tour guide broke us up into groups of five so that we could focus in on our talks and try to get to know each other better. I guess the idea was that friendships would spark, and you'd be determined to go to that college because of them. Friendships have never sparked for me.

"But your mom was in that group with me. We were all awkward – all five of us – not wanting to say anything. Then the guide told us to play a game of 'Two Truths and a Lie.' Do you know what that is?"

"Yeah, it's when you have to tell two truths about yourself and make up one lie. Then the other people in the game have to guess which one is the lie. The best liar wins the game."

"Exactly. As luck would have it, I was chosen to go first. So, I gave my lie first, to try to throw them off. Most people save the lie for last, because they forget they need to think one up, and they quickly, and transparently, throw it on at the end.

"So I lied first and said, 'I just got married after graduation, so I'll be looking to move into the married dorms.' It wasn't a bad lie. Everyone was getting married super young back then. Then I followed up with my two truths. I said, 'I currently work as a dish washer' and 'I plan on studying to become a filmmaker.' I figured everyone would think I was lying about becoming a filmmaker. It was certainly the most outlandish statement of the three. And of the four other people in our group, three of them said that was my lie. The only person who didn't was Annie. After everyone else had guessed incorrectly, she said, 'You're not married.'"

"How did she know?" I asked, becoming invested in the story.

"Look at me!" Dad says with a crusty laugh. "Aside from my haggard looks, she knew for another reason. She said, 'You're not wearing a ring.' It was such an obvious mistake on my part, and I felt incredibly dumb. But no one else even thought to look at my ring finger. They just assumed that only the craziest thing of the three could be the lie." Dad smiles to himself. "That was your mom in a nutshell. She was insightful, attentive, and just plain smart."

"Do you remember what Mom's 'Two Truths and a Lie' were?"

"Sure, I do. First, she said, 'I grew up in a rural town with a population of 114 people. Then she said, 'I have an undeclared major.' Lastly, she said, 'I am a second or third cousin to Julie Christie.' Of course, most people thought the third one was a lie, because she wasn't even sure of how closely related she was to a famous actress. For most people, if they were related to a celebrity, they would know exactly how closely related they were. Not only that, they would mention it and play it up for the rest of their lives. I, of course, knew that was her lie."

"How so?"

"I told her, 'First off, you are definitely related to Julie Christie.' One of the other group members scoffed and said, 'How could you know that?' I told the person, 'Look at her eyes. Julie Christie has those lovely, determined eyes. So does Annie.' Your mom blushed when I said that. I can still remember her face. I then said, 'So, I know your first statement is your lie. With those determined eyes, there's no way you're going into college undeclared.'"

"That's actually pretty amazing," I admitted.

"You gotta remember, I was going to school to study filmmaking. I loved movies, so I obviously knew Julie Christie's work very well. She wasn't going to get a lie over on me that easily."

I cannot help but smile. *This is him* – this is the Dad I remember loving being around as a kid. Funny, engaging, and charismatic. This is obviously the man Mom fell in love with.

Dad continues, "Before, you asked me what I talked about with your mom. 'What was the last thing you said to her?' you asked. Well," he says, opening his hands, "I said that. I told her, 'I fell in love with your eyes forty years ago, and I have never fallen out of love with them since.'"

13

When he returns, Steve is astounded to find me sitting by Dad in Mom's room. It is such a turn of events that he can only assume something even worse, medically, has happened in another one of his brief absences.

"What happened?" he says, eyes bulging.

"Nothing," I say. "We were just talking to Mom about the old times."

Steve assumes I am lying, but I nod and assure him I am not. He slowly sits down on the other side of her bed. He places his hand on the one I am not holding.

"Did Luke do okay going back to his mom so soon?" Dad asks.

"He cried," Steve shrugs, "but he does that pretty much any time one of us has to drop him off with the other. Doesn't matter which."

I know Steve thinks that, for many reasons, he should have just stayed married to Mallory, despite her affairs. No, he does not love her the way he once did, but he does love Lucas. I know he would do just about anything he could to give his son a "traditional" upbringing with both parents always around. Unfortunately, that decision was not solely Steve's to make.

Steve squeezes Mom's hand. Her head is tilted toward the window, most likely unintentionally. Her eyes are devoid of any sort of acknowledgement. In fact, they show signs of severe dryness, since she does not have the muscle strength to close them on her own after that last massive stroke. "Sorry I was gone so long, Mom," he says. "Luke had a great time seeing you, though."

He drops his head and begins to softly cry. I know the exact sensation he is feeling. We, of course, never intend to cry each time we see her again, but coming back to her like this is such a harsh reality check. It is impossible to not be moved to tears. Like me, though, Steve tries to stifle his tears. The doctors and nurses tell us that she is still capable of hearing, and we do not want her to feel sad – for either herself or on behalf of us.

"Oh, I almost forgot," Dad says, reaching into his pocket. He pulls out his phone and navigates for a few seconds. Soon, the song "Time" by Pink Floyd begins playing softly. He places it near her pillow. Dad then catches Steve and me giving him an odd look and says, "What? She likes this song. We used to dance to it in my dorm room in college."

Steve and I both unintentionally groan at the thought of our parents sharing an unsupervised space of any kind.

"Oh, grow up," Dad says.

"What's the plan for tonight?" Steve asks. "I can stay again if..."

"If it's okay with you and Dad," I begin, "I'd like to stay tonight. And then Dad can stay tomorrow."

Steve looks visibly shaken now that he is officially out of the loop. I know he is asking himself, *Why does she care what Dad wants? They were literally about to fistfight an hour ago.*

"That's okay with me," Dad says. "But I do want to stay tomorrow night. Deal?"

Steve and I both nod. It is odd, but facing the trauma of losing one of our core family members has somehow brought our family unit closer together.

"I know you guys usually go back and eat at Steve's place," Dad says, "but do you wanna stay here tonight and eat in the cafeteria with me? Their pork tenderloin sandwich is actually pretty good. After that, the Royals have the night game on ESPN."

"Sure, we could do that," I say.

Not wanting to question the ubiquitous happiness in the room any longer, Steve quickly joins in. "This is a big game tonight. Might be a decider for the division."

As the hours pass before dinnertime, Steve, Dad, and I reminisce about scores of memories. Mom is visibly incapable of showing any appreciation for how our family dynamic has so suddenly shifted and corrected itself, but I know she feels both relief and contentment.

After the Royals game (which ends in a much-needed victory), Dad and Steve leave the hospital. I pull out the recliner/bed and find a couple pillows and blankets in the closet. I prepare my bedding and turn down what lights I can operate without interfering with what the hospital staff needs for nightly check-ins.

After I get into some shorts and a tee shirt, I go and sit beside Mom. I stroke her hair, looking at the face I have known all my life and how it has not changed expression in hours. I feel so protective of her, wanting to fight all her battles in her stead, if only given the opportunity.

"Dad told me today about how you two met," I tell her. I pause, unsure if I should reveal everything in my head. I decide it's okay. "You know, I have been angry at him for so long. I always felt as though he chose his career over you – over all of us. He really made me feel unwanted. I know, deep down, that wasn't his intention and that he did love us. It just hurt then. It still does." I pause. "But as we all ate dinner tonight, I realized something. Dad couldn't have been all that bad. He couldn't have intentionally meant to hurt us... because you chose him. You loved him. You were – you *are* – a strong woman. There's no chance that you'd let a man dictate your life or neglect the children you shared." I pause again. "I guess I don't understand everything just yet, but I know I will eventually. I do know one thing, though – I love you. We all do. I am so happy that you are our mother."

I give Mom a kiss on her forehead and tell her goodnight before descending to my sleeping spot. My bed sits much lower than her hospital bed, but I still sleep with my hand craned up so that I can hold hers, at least until I fall asleep.

14

"I could hear you snoring down the hallway."

I try my best to pry my eyes open to see who is talking to me, but the back of my eyelids feel as though they are glued to my eyeballs. I know I probably look like Bill Cosby selling pudding pops when I finally come up with a coherent thought. "Huh?"

"Em, you good?" Steve says, as he starts to take shape in the bright light above me. "You're hanging halfway out of the chair."

I attempt to pull myself up, feeling every sore muscle in my torso as I do. "Yeah, I'm fine. The nursing staff just pops in and out a lot throughout the night."

"And they flick on the lights like it's nothing," he says.

I am fully awake now. I snap my head toward him. "Exactly. I mean, I know this isn't supposed to be like a fine hotel stay, but… man, they just roll in like the Gestapo."

"They do," he agrees.

I rub my eyes and throw off the paper-thin blanket that the hospital provided. *Lord knows how many people have used this…*

"Heard from Dad yet?" I ask.

"He actually made a group chat with us."

I grab my phone to look. "He did?"

"I know. Crazy."

"I didn't even think he knew how to do that."

"Well," Steve begins, "I think Dad's pretty phone savvy – just not with us."

"Fair enough," I say, rolling my eyes. "Looks like he'll be here soon. I'm gonna throw on some new clothes. You good?"

"Yeah," Steve says, turning back toward Mom. "Take your time."

I softly close the door behind me as I enter the bathroom to change my clothes. It's my outfit from two days ago – I basically live the life of Keith Richards now, except for the hard drugs. I look at myself in the foggy mirror and see something that once resembled a human female looking back at me. I run my fingers through my hair as an impromptu comb, but it only makes my hair look worse. I drop my hands. *Why do I even bother?*

I grab the door handle to leave, but I hear Steve talking to Mom. I put my ear close to the door to listen, but then I pull away, disgusted. I know I shouldn't listen to his private conversations with Mom, but I am equally curious about what their morning talks sound like. I wonder if they sound like mine – where I assure Mom of my love for her, remind her of all the good times, and give her updates about our family. I start to feel self-conscious.

Am I making Mom feel worse by having these kinds of "final" conversations?

Should I just tell her everything is okay?

Can she even hear me? Was that a lie told by the doctors and nursing staff just to make the surviving family members feel better?

Fearing that I may be worsening my mother's condition, I lean against the door and listen to my brother.

Despite how hard I try, I do not hear anything at first, but then I hear him laugh. It's only then that I feel comfortable with my decision to eavesdrop and go back into the main room.

Steve looks over at me, smiling. "I was just reminding Mom about that time she took me to a movie when I was like... six or seven." He laughs again.

I sit down next to him, at the foot of her bed. "What happened? I don't remember." Truthfully, because of my father, I have blocked out all of the movie memories of my own.

"Well, we were in Kansas City – I think we were seeing *Mighty Joe Young* – and afterwards, I had to go to the bathroom. I was right at that age where I didn't really want to go into the bathroom with her anymore. I would kind of get weird looks from the other ladies in there. Plus, I wanted to feel more independent – like I was a 'man.' Anyway, Mom agreed to let me go into the men's room on my own, but she gave me a warning first. She told me she had just seen a news story, a couple of nights before, where an unknown man came up to a kid at a urinal at a restaurant and cut off his penis. They never caught the guy or found out what his motivation was."

"Why are you laughing at that?" I gasp.

He shrugs, "Because only Mom would give that warning to a six-year-old kid going into a public bathroom for the first time on his own." He shakes his head at the memory, chuckling. "I remember walking in and being so terrified. I gripped myself as hard as I could before I got to the urinal, and I tried to relieve myself as quickly as I possibly could – before someone else entered the bathroom.

And someone did. I remember some guy came in and stood at a urinal three or four down from me. I didn't want to stare at him, but I knew it was the guy... *the Circumciser*."

"Is that what they actually called him on the news?"

"No, that's just the name I came up for him over the years. In my head, I built him up into this terrible horror villain. Sure, Freddy haunts your dreams, but the Circumciser goes right for the gold. He grabs ya brusquely, extends ya, and then... whack! After that, he's off to find another."

"What is wrong with you, Steve?"

He smiles. "I dunno. My storytelling must come from Dad."

"Okay, well in this 'Circumciser' series, why does he whack off...?"

"Poor choice of words."

"Sorry. Why does he collect so many... dongles?"

"'Dongles?' Isn't that the old converter thing for an iPhone?"

"Yeah..."

"Why do you call penises 'dongles'?"

"I dunno. Penis just sounds so... *graphic*."

"It's literally the least graphic name for it. It's anatomy."

"I don't like it."

"You don't like the word or penises in general?"

"Can you please stop?" I plead. "I don't feel comfortable talking about... *dongles*... with my brother."

"Well, you asked the question about the Circumciser," he reminds.

"Yes, but just because it was so stupid."

"Oh, so it's a stupid story?"

"Ugh," I nearly scream. He laughs at his success to get on my nerves. "I was just curious as to how far you had taken this nightmarish scenario in your head. That's all."

"I see."

We sit in silence for a moment. He raises his eyebrows. Finally, I erupt, "Well, tell me!"

Steve leans in, as if Mom's bed were a campfire. "So, the Circumciser is on the lookout for the exact... *dongle*... that he remembers from his childhood."

I furrow my brow, and then the realization hits me. "Ooooh... Wow, Steve that's... dark."

"Well, the thing is, Bradley's neighbor..."

"Who's Bradley?"

"That's the Circumciser's real name before he turned bad."

"Oh," I say, as if any of this makes sense.

"So, anyway, Bradley's neighbor tried to attack him when he was just a boy – six or seven."

"Like you," I say, eyes widening, feeding into his story.

"*Exactly*. But Bradley was hip to what the old neighbor was up to. He saw him spying through his front room windows every summer after Memorial Day."

"Why the front room?"

"Because they lived across the street from a public pool. Well, it was actually two streets, separated by a median."

I cannot handle much more of his nonsense, and he knows it. "Of course."

"Bradley knew he was a creeper, even though he had no frame of reference for what a child molester, killer, or kidnapper would look like or how he would act. He just knew that the old man with poor vision next door was bad news. On one particular day, Bradley was out riding his bike in the driveway when he saw the old man looking over the wooden fence between their yards. Without a doubt, the old man was looking *right at him*. Bradley started to peddle toward his house, but the old man beckoned him over. 'Hey, Bradley!' he shouted over the fence. 'Come here for a sec.' Bradley looked at his house, and he knew no one was home. He was a latchkey kid."

"A 'latchkey kid'?" I interrupt.

"This happened in the 1970s," Steve continued, convinced that he had actually created a truth. "So, he knows no one is home to protect him. What's he supposed to do? If he runs home, the old man would just find a way in. He probably knew how late Bradley's mother worked, too. It was clear to young Bradley that the old man had been casing his house."

"What about Bradley's dad?"

"He died in Vietnam. Well, specifically he died in Cambodia during the Vietnam War. A helicopter crash. Killed five others as well. Bradley was only four."

"How tragic," I say, actually feeling sorry for the imaginary boy who would later grow up to become a serial dongle-whacker.

"It was. He didn't realize it at the time, but Bradley later understood that PTSD played a huge part in his actions later in life."

"Well, stick to the early parts right now."

"Right," Steve nods, getting back on track. "With no options, Bradley walks up to the fence where the old man stood. He maintained eye contact with him the whole time. Once he got closer – enough to see his own reflection in the Coke-bottle-thick eyeglasses of the old man – he asked him, 'What do you need?' The old man grunted a bit and then said, 'Can you help me with this?' Bradley looked at him, dumbfounded, and asked, 'With what?' The old man then peered over his glasses and nodded downward. Bradley's eyes followed the old man's eyeline until he discovered what he was speaking about. The geezer had stuck his dried-out, liver-spotted pecker through a hole in the wooden fence. Fearful, Bradley looked up again as the old man repeated, 'Can you help me with this?' Bradley looked down, but he wasn't looking at John's wang. Instead, Bradly was searching his immediate area. He slowly bent down as the old man closed his eyes, who expected that his perverse plan had finally paid off. But Bradley wasn't crouching down for the wrinkly ramrod – he was searching for a weapon. Bradley grabbed a small hand machete from the damp grass. Its blade was rusted over from too many nights in the open rain. Bradley then reigned down upon the trouser snake with a forceful strike. The old man fell backward from the fence as his evil appendage slithered its way through the hole in the fence on Bradley's side."

    I am never one to be struck silent, but my brother's story has finally broken me. When Steve sees that I have no clarifying questions, he continues on.

    "So, from that day forward, Bradley became the Circumciser – a boy, then a teen, and then a man – who sought out the worse scum of the Earth and relieved them of their sinful devices."

    Steve leans back in his chair and smiles.

"I... How.... So, the Circumciser is a *good guy*?" I finally settle on.

"He's a vigilante, I suppose, along the lines of the Punisher or Batman. Taking the law into his own hands."

"Literally," I mutter. "Okay, so in your mind then, why would the Circumciser attack you at a urinal then when you were six years old?"

"Well, he wouldn't have, of course," Steve scoffs. "I didn't know his full backstory then."

"You mean you hadn't *made up* his backstory by then."

"Exactly. All I heard was a second-hand story from the local news about a 'mad man.' You know how the news like to report on the salacious for viewership? 'If it bleeds, it leads.' Nothing bleeds more than a man whose dongle has been chopped off."

"But Mom was the one who told you the story!" I shout, feeling insane.

"She was just a victim of the corrupt news. It wasn't her fault. We all are at a certain point in our lives."

We stare at each other until we finally erupt with laughter. "You are insane," I finally say.

"Thank you."

"When did you come up with that full story?"

"I probably pieced it all together by the time I was in middle school."

"And all from a random warning from our mother about keeping a look-out out for strangers..."

"Exactly," he smiles. He looks over at her and then says, "I know that probably sounds like the weirdest story ever to tell to a person's mother, but I know Mom would have loved it. You and I both get our warped sense of humor from her."

"We sure do," I say, smiling at her. I place a hand on her covered foot. Her face has not moved since I arrived this morning, but Steve is right – I know she is laughing on the inside. And, in a strange way, I bet she is proud that she could have inspired such insane stupidity in Steve. It's one of the many reasons we love her.

"That guy who came into the bathroom in the theater that day..." I say, thinking back.

Steve shrugs. "Just some dude. But Mom had me on my toes, that's for sure."

"Did you ever think of taglines for the 'Circumciser' film franchise?" I ask.

"Sure," Steve says. "Quite a few actually. My favorite was probably, 'Whack it and he'll whack you.' Simple, but tells the whole story."

"How about," I add, "'He takes penis envy to a whole new level.'"

"Or," Steve joins in, "'He won't tolerate any pricks.'"

"Oh, excellent," I acknowledge. "You could even publicize the first film internationally by adding or taking away footage from the movie and calling it 'The European Cut.'"

"That's good," Steve nods. "Very good."

"Maybe re-do the *Nightmare on Elm Street* chant with him instead?" I suggest. "One, two, Circumciser's coming for you..."

Steve continues, "Three, four, better close your barn door."

"Five, six, hide your chubbed-up stick."

"Seven, eight, better not masturbate."

"Nine, ten, never expose again."

We erupt in laughter again. It's so juvenile and childish, and we both know it. But that's what siblings do, especially ones like Steve and me. We get through the tough times with bizarre, inappropriate humor.

"What's all this laughing? I could hear you two from the hallway."

As soon as we hear Dad speak, we silence ourselves like we just got busted giggling in the middle of a church service. Then, realizing that Steve and I are both in our thirties, I find courage. "Oh, we were just sharing old stories with Mom."

Dad never really understood our relationship with Mom – the weird thoughts and dark humor – and that odd dynamic exists to this day. I'm beginning to understand why it's so difficult to have only one parent in your life. Part of your personality dies along with that parent unless you push to preserve that uniqueness you shared.

Dad looks down at her. He's not ready for laughter, just as we never are the first time we enter her room for the day either.

"We'll leave you two alone for a minute," Steve says, standing up. He looks at me and gestures toward the door.

"Thanks," Dad mutters.

As I close the door silently behind me, I watch as he sits in the chair closest to her and bows his head.

15

"You think he's upset with us?" Steve asks once we find ourselves in the hospice lobby again.

"Nah, he knows how we get when we're together. Plus, he has no right to get onto us."

"Why? Because we're almost middle-aged?"

"No. Well, yes, that and the fact he still has a lot of explaining to do for himself," I say. "Don't get me wrong, I'm glad we are able to communicate and get along with him more now – *especially* now – but he has still been absent for a lot of Mom's hospital stay. And with all the phone calls... Something's up."

"I'll bring it up today."

I am thoroughly shocked. Steve is always the peacemaker – the one person who will do anything to keep the family from fighting or from even having the slightest confrontation. "*You'll* bring it up? That might anger him, ya know..."

"Maybe," he acknowledges, "but you're right. He does have a few things to answer for, and we can't just let that go. We know it's not right, and we will be resentful if we don't ask what he's been up to."

"Wow."

"What?"

"It's just... You're a good big brother."

Steve smiles and gives me a side hug. "Thanks, little Sis."

I give him a second before pushing off. "Don't touch me."

We walk back into the room and find Dad in the chair that visitors use most often when only one visitor in the room – the one right near the head of her bed, on the side where her motionless head rests. He does not look up when we enter, so I immediately feel as though we have returned too soon. Steve picks up on the feeling as well.

"Do you need some more time?" he asks.

"No," Dad says, still staring down at the bed, at nothing in particular. After a moment of uncomfortable silence, he says, "What was so funny earlier?"

Steve and I share a side glance, unsure of how to answer, feeling as though we have been caught smoking pot in the attic or something.

"It really wasn't anything..." Steve begins.

"I just don't understand," Dad says, finally looking up at us. "How you can find any joy right now?"

"*Excuse me*," I say sharply. I feel Steve's presence beside me tighten up like a dog owner tightening his grip on his rabid pet's leash, but it's too late. I'm off.

Looks like I'll be the one handling all of the awkward conversations today after all.

Dad shoots me a glare. "Don't get a tone with me, Little..."

"You have *no* right to judge how Steve and I handle this situation with Mom. Want to know why, Dad? Because we've *been* here. The whole time. Where the hell have you been? Showing up at the eleventh hour like some sort of lovelorn hero. Give me a break." I speak in such a flurry, I wonder if anyone understands my words at all. Then, for good measure, I spit out, "Poser."

Dad stands up with great discomfort – his leg seems to be giving him a tougher time than usual – and he silently walks toward us. "Not in here, in front of her," he demands sternly. "Lobby."

The way we are shuffled between Mom's room and the lobby, whether at the request of nurses, doctors, or Dad, is beginning to make me feel like a shackled prisoner looking forward to yard time. Once we're in the hospice lobby, we separate into our usual spots. We, however, do not sit down. This is a standing sort of conversation.

The three of us silently glance at each other, one to the other, like the leads in *The Good, the Bad, and the Ugly*, until I finally pull my gun first. *Why shouldn't I?* I'm finding my newfound bravery empowering.

"Let's get to it," I say. "Where have you been? Where is your head at?"

"My head is here – with your mother," he says without hesitation.

"Bullshit," I accuse. "You show up to the hospital later than us every single day. You leave earlier than us every single day. And oftentimes, when we can't find you, you're off in a corner or in the cafeteria or in outside lobby on the phone. So, what, for you, is taking precedence over Mom's final moments on this Earth?"

Dad breathes a deep, labored sigh. He knows there is no refuting what I have just pointed out. He glances at Steve. I'm not sure why. Maybe he thinks he will find some sort of refuge with his other, older child, but Steve stands firmly with me, and Dad clearly sees that. "I was offered a job," he finally says. Knowing that he has officially lost the Mexican stand-off, he plops down with a groan.

"What job?" Steve says, following suit. I do as well, but with protest in my mind. I want to stand up and fight, physically and verbally.

"A directing gig."

"You're retired," Steve says, shaking his head. "You don't make movies anymore."

"No, I don't," he agrees. "This job is unique, though."

"We've heard that one before," I mutter. "He said it every time he left us for months at a time."

"They're releasing Eric Davis from prison."

Steve and I look at each other. Even I have to acknowledge the magnitude of this news. Davis was the subject behind Dad's biggest documentary, *Out of Mind*. It launched his entire career.

And ended his time with us.

16

To understand Dad's career, you first have to understand a little schlocky horror movie called *Killer Be Killed*.

Killer Be Killed was a no-budget horror movie directed by a man named Eric Davis. A little older than Dad when he struck a similar height of fame, Davis hit it big for all the wrong reasons. You see, low budget horror movies were common in the 1970s, but "found footage" movies were not. Today, these types of movies are everywhere (*The Blair Witch Project*, *Paranormal Activity*, *REC*, and plenty more), but audiences were not privy to the moviemakers' tactics at the time. If a movie felt that realistic, let alone "found" by accident, then it was assumed the movie was real.

The controversy surrounding Davis's movie centered around a girl who was supposedly killed while filming was underway. Of course, she was not actually killed, but she was in the "film" and her whereabouts after filming were unknown. Because of the weird coincidences outside the filmmaking of *Killer Be Killed*, it was assumed (by audiences, critics, and even industry insiders) that Davis had actually made a snuff film and had actually killed her onscreen. To make matters worse in the court of public opinion, the missing girl suffered a terrible death involving torture. One particularly memorable scene involved newspaper twine.

Because they couldn't find the actress in real life (her real name was Charlie Woods), Eric Davis was arrested for murder. After a speedy, and very public, trial, he was sentenced to a minimum of twenty-five years in prison. He probably would have received a life sentence, or even the death penalty, had the case against him had a *shred* of evidence.

Dad, being an enormous movie fan, was smitten with Davis's case and set out to find the truth behind the making of the movie. Dad assumed, like everyone else, that Charlie Woods had been killed, but he soon came to believe that Davis was actually innocent. Sensing a story worthy of a feature-length documentary, Dad ended up making *Out of Mind* about the whole fiasco. His documentary was not only an enormous critical and commercial success, but it changed the public mindset in regarding Eric Davis.

Dad proved himself to be a trailblazer. Because of the success of *Out of Mind*, advocacy documentaries really took off in the 1980s and '90s, with films like *The Thin Blue Line, Paradise Lost,* and *The Staircase* following suit.

The news of Davis's release can only mean one thing for us.

Dad is about to leave us again.

17

"They're releasing Eric Davis because of your film?"

Steve is just as blown away as I am. "But you made *Out of Mind* decades ago."

"His case was re-examined after several thousand letters of petitioning," Dad explains. "Seems interest in the case grew after those true crime docs took off on Netflix."

"The genre you basically invented." Steve pauses and then asks, "They want you to do a film about his release? Like an epilogue sort of thing?"

"Exactly."

"What did you say to them?"

Dad turns slowly to face me. "I told them 'no.'"

Even I'm shocked by that revelation. "And?" Steve pries again.

"Well, based on the number of phone calls you've seen me take while spying on me," he says out of the corner of his mouth, "you can imagine that they're pretty desperate to get me involved. Forget movies – this will be one of the biggest news stories of the year."

"This is big," Steve acknowledges. "Did you tell the producers why you said 'no'?"

"I told Rusty I had a family matter to attend to."

Rusty Martin was Dad's producer for all of his documentaries over the years. He was also Dad's best friend and a symbol of departure for us. If Rusty showed up on our doorstep, no matter what time of day or what day of the year, Dad was sure to be leaving the house within minutes.

"You should have been more specific," Steve says, somewhat irritated. "I'm sure they would have been more understanding."

"And made fewer calls," I add snidely.

Dad only shrugs. "Not their business."

"So what happened anyway?" Steve asks. "With Davis I mean. And that girl."

Dad takes a breath. "Charlie Woods was just discovered in Florida. The story emerging is that she was kidnapped in New Mexico right after *Killer Be Killed* wrapped production in '74. She, along with six other 'missing children' from that era, were finally uncovered this week. Their identities were just verified today."

"That's exactly what you theorized in *Out of Mind*," Steve says, staring off. "That she was abducted and taken out of state."

Dad nods. "That lunatic who kidnapped all of those kids was keeping them in his own man-made dungeon underneath his trailer."

"The photograph," I say, piecing it together.

"Exactly. The photograph that we found is what finally provided the evidence about where he was keeping them. Although that photo was found in Texas, it matched scenery in Florida. The photo of Charlie, and the other missing teens and kids, was taken several months after she had been kidnapped. Apparently, our psycho friend liked to travel with images of his 'trophies' he kept back at home."

"I can't believe they're going to release him," Steve says. It is clear in his voice that he has found a whole new level of pride in Dad. But it's not just pride. It's validation. It's relief. "*Your* movie did that. When's he getting out?"

"The judge is looking over the new evidence today. We have no idea when any decision will be made, but I can't imagine that it'd take more than a couple of days. Davis has been wrongly incarcerated for decades... They are going to want to get him out as soon as possible. News on the case is literally breaking every hour – hence the incessant phone calls."

"Isn't there a younger, 'rebooted' version of you who could take over for you?" I ask.

Steve shoots me a look. "Dad's career was made based on this case, Em."

"Oh, I'm aware."

"The dude's got to be in his sixties by now... If dad made another documentary..."

"Wait a minute, Steve," Dad attempts.

"...it would be the biggest capper to a film series ever. This would cement your legacy forever!"

Dad leans back into his chair and looks at the ceiling. He chuckles.

"What, Dad?" Steve asks. His anger has dwindled. My anger, however, likes to inhabit its host (me) for a longer gestation period, like the parasite it is. I am not ready to comfort him yet.

"Nothing. It's just... funny."

"What's so funny?" I ask, mimicking his exact words from earlier.

Dad immediately picks up on what I am doing, but he doesn't give in to my taunt. "It's just funny how your views on 'legacy' change as the years pass."

"What do you mean?" Steve asks.

"I thought my legacy – that the thing I would leave behind, that would be of greatest value to me, that would show my true worth – was my filmmaking career. Specifically, *Out of Mind*. But now..." Dad trails off, still looking at the ceiling, "I realize how wrong I was."

He leans forward in his chair. "That's what's cruel about this life," he tells us. "It takes the exact amount of years we live before we can understand what our legacy really means – why we lived in the first place."

18

Dad begins talking more than I have ever heard him talk at once in a single sitting. Based on that fact alone, my anger dissipates and I listen intently, trying to figure out why it is that now, out of all the times in our lives, is the time he is willing to speak to and advise us like a father should.

"I've been obsessed with the idea of legacy for a long time now. Since I was a teenager. That's why I always kept track of my heroes' accomplishments, as well as the ages at which these heroes accomplished those feats. Even though I was a filmmaker, my most admired hero in life is Ernest Hemingway. You guys know that. He was a working writer for a long time before he wrote his first novel, but he published that first book, *The Sun Also Rises*, when he was 27. So, as soon as I became a 'professional' creator, that was my goal. By the time I was 27, I not only needed to make my first film, but it had to be one of merit – maybe not something as great as *The Sun Also Rises,* but still something that I could really be proud of. And I did.

"I made my first documentary, *Dealing Under the Stars*, when I was 25. You know, drug dealing was a big deal at drive-in movies at the time. I would know – I was there every weekend. So when I saw how often those exchanges occurred, I quickly took all of the money I had saved and bought a 16mm film camera and, bravely, I might add, secretly shot footage of the drug deals as they happened. Then, once I had enough courage, I approached some of the customers and interviewed them. I was surprised at how candid they were. As soon as I assured the users I wasn't a cop, I couldn't get them to shut up. After a couple of months, I knew I probably had enough footage for a feature, but I knew the overall movie was still lacking.

"If I didn't interview the actual drug dealers themselves, my film was lifeless. They were the spark I needed to make my film unique. So, posing as a customer, I approached several of them, night after night, week after week. I finally built up a rapport with a few of them, after I told them I was a filmmaker. People get really excited about that kind of thing. In fact, they kinda took me in as one of their own. They started calling me 'Hollywood.' After a few weeks of getting chum with them, I asked them about doing some on-camera interviews. Of course, they were hesitant at first, but once again, as soon as I assured them I wasn't really a filmmaker-cop, they were willing to tell me anything. Everything.

"*Dealing Under the Stars* launched my career, for sure. I made several films in between, but I never felt like I achieved the level of competence that Hemingway did, even at a younger age. Frankly, I still don't think I ever have. But the closest I got was with *Out of Mind*. I shot it when I was 33. That's when everything changed.

"I wanted my life to mean something, so that's why I pushed myself *so* hard creatively and why I was *so* hard on myself when I saw myself as failing. That's also why I was so work-driven and... *absent*. When I was that age, I could only think, 'I will never direct a movie as good as *Raging Bull*. I will never write poetry as good as 'Strawberry Fields

Forever.' And I certainly will never write a book as good as *A Farewell to Arms*.

"Your mom never cared about those things. While I was obsessed with my legacy, she was focused primarily on raising you two. And her efforts had to be doubled, not just because there were two of you, but because I wasn't there most of the time. She loved you both so deeply and passionately. After a while, with me being gone so much, it became clear that you had taken over most of her heart. There wasn't much room left for me. But that was my own fault. Instead of correcting myself or my selfish behavior, though, I forged ahead even harder with my career.

"*Out of Mind* became my *Citizen Kane*. I'm not comparing my film to Welles's masterpiece, but I could not get out from under *Mind's* shadow, just like Orson couldn't escape *Kane*. Nothing was ever as good – for either of us. And I tried desperately to top *Mind*.

"As odd as it sounds, I was doing it for you. You may not believe me, but in the back of my head, I was so worried that when you two became adults, you'd be ashamed of my work – ashamed that I never achieved a level of greatness like Hemingway's. All kids become ashamed of their parents by the time they hit a certain age. It's inevitable, and I always knew that would be the case with my own kids. I just didn't want you to feel *that way* toward me your whole life.

"Instead of asking myself, 'Will Steve and Emma be upset with me for not directing as well as Scorsese?' I should have been asking myself, 'Am I putting all of my efforts into making films to earn other peoples' attention, to the detriment of my own kids?' I never switched those two questions around, because I knew the answer would be too hard for me to swallow.

"I know I'm talking a lot here, and you're probably getting tired of your old man's analogies, but here's another reason I look at things differently now. In 1974, John Lennon was asked if he had any regrets in his life. He probably had several potential answers – getting addicted to (and then kicking) heroin in 1969, the poor mixing on one of his favorite songs ('Across the Universe'), and, obviously, being the instigator behind the dissolution of the world's greatest band. But when he thought it over, he came up with an unexpected answer. He recalled his son from his first marriage – the son Lennon had basically abandoned. Lennon said, 'If I had this time over, I'd be different to Julian.' In other words, he wasn't most regretful of letting himself down bodily, letting himself down artistically, or, on an enormous scale, letting down the world. Instead, he was most regretful of letting down his son, Julian. John Lennon went through a lot of trial and errors before he came to that realization. So did I.

"For most people, legacy means what we are able to accomplish for our friends and family. It's how they will remember us. In my head, I wasn't 'most people.' I had to achieve a greater legacy so the entire world wouldn't forget about me after I was dead."

He pauses.

"And then all of this happened. With your mom. Her cancer. Her late diagnosis. That changed my thinking overnight. Your mom never tried to be a John Lennon, but she *did* try to be a good parent – something even the great

John Lennon, one of my greatest heroes, wished he had been better at.

"That's when I realized I wanted your mother's idea of legacy instead of my own. Deep down, in the pit of my stomach, I knew you kids loved your mother more than you loved me, even though I worked harder at my career than she had to work at being a great mother. But if you loved her more, what did it matter? Why did I try so hard? In trying to win your 'future' approval, I was actually losing your current love and respect. Without that, there would never be any future love for me.

"That's why I have been turning down all of these film offers, even though it's the greatest possible thing that could happen to my career. Not only would it bring me out of, essentially forced, retirement, but also people would view me as 'great' once again. My filmography would have a nice coda at the end – what every serious artist wants. All of that is true. But at what cost?

"I have turned down every offer because I wanted you both to know that, even in my old-ass state, I willingly made a change. I put you first. *Finally*. Decades too late. You two, and your mother, are my foremost priorities now. Maybe that means I am putting myself out of my comfort zone, which is all but reclusive now. It doesn't matter what it is – if you need me, or she needs me, then I'll be there. I'm sorry you think I have been absent, especially during these past few terrible days. I have attempted to do just the opposite of that, however. Since your mother's diagnosis, I have vowed to try and better myself in every way I can. Not with filmmaking, though – with you guys.

"I know that my struggles might seem unique to some, even to you. I may dwell on certain ideas for years, while other people may come to satisfactory conclusions to the same problems in the amount of time it takes them to peel an apple. What we all have in common, though, is that whatever our problems are, they will never end. In fact, they will only accumulate each year. It's quite discouraging when you think about it.

"That was certainly true of my hero. Hemingway spent his life writing great books – perhaps *the* greatest. But how did it all end? With depression, anguish, and loneliness. Hemingway's father, Clarence, shot and killed himself when he was 57 years old. Hemingway did outlast his father's lifespan, but not by much. He shot himself when he was 61 years old."

He pauses again.

"Was that really my goal? To create great work, but then be so wrought with despair that I die unhappy and prematurely? Again, I started to see things from your perspective. Would you rather have a father you barely knew, who made documentaries that people respected, or would you rather have a father, albeit years too late, who was simply there for you and gave you the care when you needed it? Especially after… well, you know. Her diagnosis.

"George Harrison said, 'Try to realize it's all within yourself, no one else can make you change.' You may not find the answer to life's problems within yourself necessarily, but within yourself, you may discover where you need to look."

He smiles.

"Turns out, I just needed to look at you two."

19

Steve stands, walks to a nearby snack station, grabs a bottle of water, and hands it to Dad. The urgency with which he does so is akin to supplying a desert-traveling cowboy a much-needed final drink from a canteen.

"Thanks, Son," Dad says after he gulps nearly the whole bottle. He stops drinking when the bottle begins to crumble inward and crunch.

"I have literally never heard you talk so much," Steve says, "in thirty-plus years."

"It's weird," Dad says, "these are things I've meant to say to you two for a long time, but… I dunno."

"Why didn't you?" I ask.

He shrugs. "I guess I was scared."

"You interviewed and hung out with legitimate criminals in your career – drug dealers, murderers, rapists…" I say, "but you were afraid of *us*? Your own kids?"

"My generation was different," Dad says. "Men didn't open up like this. We thought and felt certain things, but we never spoke them out loud. We just tried to express those deeper emotions with a head nod or a tussle of the hair." His eyes shift, surveying the room. "Still, it was tough to talk to you because… well, you two and your mother are the only ones who really matter to me."

"Isn't that the big reason *to talk* to us then?"

"You'd think so," he agrees. "Life's weird like that. You can open up to complete strangers, but when it comes to your own family, you sometimes have trouble finding the right words – any words – that show how you feel. Sometimes in the past, when I attempted to have this conversation with you two, it felt as though my vocal chords would lock up. I have no idea why. Maybe I was afraid of what reaction I might get. Or of feeling too vulnerable. Who knows?"

"Have you opened up to Mom yet?" Steve asks.

"Each day, I go into her room and tell her everything I need to," he says. "I tell her things I've neglected to tell her in the past, things I wanted for us in the future, and, of course, things I have always felt about her." Dad's face convulses as if speaking so open-heartedly has caused his nervous system to deteriorate. His internal system knows something is off. "I love your mother. I always have. No, I wasn't the greatest at showing it or at always being there when she needed me, but that was because of my own issues – my obsession with work. My poor behavior was never a reflection of how I felt about her."

A sense of relief, for all three of us, seems to have enveloped the room and comforted us. I may still have my issues with Dad, but I no longer feel actively angry at him. As misguided as he was at times, I do now understand why he was the way he was. Part of me is jealous that he was so driven. I cannot seem to find the drive to do anything, other than be here for Mom at her worst moment.

"We should get back in there," Dad says. "I don't like her being alone for too long."

"Yeah," Steve says, standing. "What's the plan for tonight, Em? You or me?"

"You talking about who's staying overnight here?"

"Oh," Steve suddenly stops himself, "sorry, I didn't mean to exclude you. I just figured…"

"If it's okay with you both, I would like to be the 'night man' tonight," Dad says.

"Are you sure?" I ask. "That fold out chair-bed is not the most comfortable…"

"I'll be fine. I camped out in the jungle for eight weeks during the mid-eighties."

I remember that, I think. *That's when you missed my birthday,* and *Thanksgiving, to track down an old plane from a downed World War II hero.* I decide not to remind him of my still-bitter memory, though.

"As much as I've already said today," Dad says, "there's still a lot more I need to say to her."

The rest of the day was, surprisingly, one of the best our family ever spent together, despite the fact Mom could not respond. If she had been in a different physical state, it would have been the greatest day of my life probably. As it was, however, we had a great time reminiscing about the (few) good times we shared during our childhood, and Steve and I informed Dad about some of our more wild antics. As our parent, he was disturbed in part, even disappointed, but the other part of him was humored by our revelations.

Still, I felt a sense of melancholy while telling those stories. I could sense that Dad wanted to have been there – to have been more involved in our lives. I had never seen guilt so present on his face. It was clear to me that, if given the chance now, he would have spent his time at my lame birthday party and not in the dangerous jungle looking for a war hero's corpse.

Once again, I could not help but notice a recurring theme throughout our discussions. It seems as though we always think we know what we want out of life... until it's too late to shift our priorities to what we really desire.

I hope I am able to remember that.

We ate lunch and dinner alongside Mom's bed (Steve brought back fast food for lunch; I brought up cafeteria food for dinner), and after that, we watched some sports highlights. It was then I noticed the time and how quickly the day had slid away.

"It's ten o'clock, Steve," I said. "We better get out of here."

Dad stood with his usual groan and said, "Rest up. I'll see you sometime tomorrow. Your mom and I will be fine."

"We'll be here early," Steve insists.

"Whatever time you get here is fine," Dad says, before adding, "but could you bring me a coffee from that gas station across the street when you do? You think they'd be expert coffee makers around this place, but it's all gruel."

Steve smiles. "Sure thing."

I give Dad a hug and say, "See you in the morning."

20

"Emma, wake up!"

"Ezekiel?!" I shout, lunging forward in the tiny bed. I throw the dinosaur to the floor.

"Em, you gotta get up," Steve insists.

"What's going on?" I ask, searching the bed for my phone while also trying to adjust my eyes to the darkness. "What time is it?"

"It's 1:40," Steve says. "Dad just called. Mom's blood pressure has dropped. *A lot.* The attending nurse said that immediate family should come as soon as possible."

"Shit, okay," I say, flustered. "I'll throw my clothes on."

"I'm gonna start the car," he says, running out. "I'll meet you outside."

Within four minutes, Steve and I are speeding down the streets of downtown Kansas City, twenty miles per hour over the limit. I have never seen the city streets so empty, and with no policemen present. It is as if a heavenly presence were clearing the way for our arrival.

Steve and I do not speak. I'm not sure what he is thinking about, but in my head, I am running through every worst-case scenario. I am remembering playing with Mom when I was a little girl. I am remembering arguing with her in high school. I am remembering when we found out about her cancer diagnosis. I am remembering the last time I heard her speak.

It seems obvious. This is the morning we are going to say goodbye.

Because of the early hour, Steve and I have to enter the hospital through the emergency entrance, alongside gunshot victims and people clearly freaking out on bad drug trips. We slither past them all and approach a policeman who guards the entry to the main section of the hospital. We hand over our driver's licenses, and he prints off sticky name tags for us. Once that obnoxious ordeal is done, we bolt through the hallway of the first floor of the hospital and dash to the hospice house.

"Kids," Dad exhales upon seeing us. I have never seen him so distraught. He has clearly been crying, and he is showing signs of anxiety that I know all too well. I've been in such a rush this morning that I just haven't even had a chance to let my own anxiety take hold of me yet, but I know it's coming, and my medication is somewhere under Ezekiel, I believe.

We look at Mom – and we hug Dad. Two nurses hover in the room, monitoring her, and a doctor is popping in and out of the room. Words are spoken, data is being recorded, but I can't seem to focus on anything but her – lying still in that bed, with her head tilted to the side, laboriously breathing.

That's my mom.

"Could you say that again?" I hear Steve say, and I snap out of my daze.

"Her blood pressure right now is dangerously low," says a doctor I've never met before.

"Does that...?" Steve begins. No one knows for sure what words he thought about saying, but we all knew what question he was about to ask.

The doctor saves Steve the heartbreak of voicing his thoughts out loud. "You never know what will happen in this type of situation, but given the numbers and my experience, I'd say this is probably it."

I freeze in place. Dad's eyes shoot to the floor. Steve begins to cry.

"There's no change right now," one of the nurses, who is also new to me, says. She then turns to us and says, "We'll give you some time with her and then be back in shortly. If you need us at all, just push that button." She points to the big red button above the hospital bed.

The two nurses and doctor mutter their goodbyes – condolences, I'm not sure. All I know is that the room is soon empty, and it's just the four of us again.

The room is silent and dark. No light filters through the main window; the only light glowing is a small one right above Mom's headboard, providing a halo effect. No one speaks. The only sound comes from the machines monitoring her life functions.

After standing still for a few minutes that feel like hours, Dad finally speaks. "I think... we, uh, need..."

He cannot finish his thought. It is too painful for him to tell his children that they should say goodbye to their mother.

"Yeah," Steve agrees. "I think so."

The three of us grab chairs and place ourselves around her bed. Dad, as usual, is at the top, right by her head. He claims the side to which her face tilts. Steve grabs one of her hands, and I grab the other.

The touch of her hand already feels so much different. It's nearly devoid of any warmth. Purple mottling is overtaking the topside of it. A nurse already told us that mottling indicates a person is at the end of life. Mom's hand feels softer than usual as well, and there is no sense of reciprocation when I grab hold of it. It just feels lifeless.

Where are you? It's Em...

I look up from her hand and see that Dad is whispering something in her ear. I cannot decipher what he is saying, and, frankly, I don't want to know. It's only meant for her ears. On the opposite side of the bed, Steve holds her other hand tightly as he sobs.

I look back to her left hand – the one I am holding. I caress it with my thumb, just to indicate to her that I am still here, even though she cannot hear my voice because I am speechless, crushed, and full of despair. I knew this moment would come, but I never thought it would come so suddenly.

I lean down and kiss her hand and then speak to it. I know it doesn't make sense, but still, I feel as though she can hear me in some way. "I love you, Mom," I say. As soon as I speak, I begin to cry as well. That's the thing with me. I can bottle up my emotions, until it's finally time to use my words. After I regain some composure, I continue. "I know this is probably the last time I'll speak to you, at least on this Earth. I just want you to know how much you meant to all of us – me, Steve, Dad, Lucas... *everyone*. We all love you so much." I pause to find strength to say the following words. "I don't want you to be in pain any longer. If this is your time to go, then..."

I can't. I cannot tell my mother it is okay for her to let go, because it isn't. I am not okay with it. I know it's selfish, and the life she is currently living is not sustainable, but I want her to exist in any form that she can. I want her in my life still.

I wipe my tears away before I look up. My dad and brother seem to be saying their goodbyes as well. A wave of depression overtakes me as I see my family in such shared pain. *How are we ever going to function after all of this?*

One of the new nurses enters again, and the three of us slowly back away from the bed to give her room to check on Mom.

"Any changes?" Dad asks.

"Her blood pressure is still very low," the nurse answers. "No changes to speak of. I'll be back in soon."

I watch her leave and feel defeated. The constant no news/same situation thing has been happening for days, and it is wearing me down to my core. I don't want to say goodbye to my mother, yet I feel as though the hospital staff constantly makes me start the process over and over again from scratch.

But if that's what I've got to do, then that's what I'll do.

The darkness hovers in the room as the three of us weep silently and say goodbye to the heart of our family.

21

I feel heat on the side of my face as I attempt to pry my eyes open.

Sunlight.

I fell asleep. How could I have fallen asleep?!

I jerk my head up from the backrest of the chair and see that Steve is also asleep. Dad seems as though he has just awakened. I look at Mom, who appears to look exactly as she did when Steve and I ran in at two o'clock this morning.

"What's the status?" I ask Dad. "What's going on with her?"

"No change," he says. "Actually, she's doing better now."

"*Better?*"

"Her blood pressure stabilized, and she's no longer in that danger zone she was in this morning."

I shake my head, unable to comprehend. *But I already said goodbye to her?*

"I know," Dad says, "it really felt as though this morning was going to be it."

Just then, Steve begins to stir. I see a familiar franticness. He is as perplexed as I am. As Dad repeats the exact words he said to me just seconds ago, I duck into the bathroom.

I flick on the light and stare at myself in the mirror. I look, feel, and, probably, smell gross. I examine the circles under my eyes. I feel resentment – not toward Mom or the doctors and nurses for the false alarm this morning, but for being able to so easily walk into a bathroom and feel anything.

I stare at myself in the mirror a moment longer and then an urge takes over. I slap myself hard across the face. I "tell" myself that my aggressive intent is to wake myself up from one of the most restless nights of my life, but that's not true.

I slap myself again, even harder. I do it because I want to feel physical pain instead of emotional pain. It's so much easier.

I slap myself a third and final time, as hard as I possibly can. The pain causes tears to instantly run down my face.

Good. That's better.

If she can't be without pain, then neither should I.

At about noon, Steve and I finally leave the hospice wing. Dad assures us he is fine – he brought clothes from home and can shower in the communal bathroom – so after much prodding on his behalf, we finally leave.

We don't want to leave her again, but we both need a restart. We need something positive so we can better be there for Mom and Dad. In an unusual show of kindness, Steve's ex-wife is allowing him an impromptu visit with Lucas. So Steve is going to take his son to a park for some sunshine and some much-needed father-son time. As for my "break," I decide to go back to Steve's place. I want to go for a run to try to clear my head, in a positive, healthy way.

When I get to Steve's house (he drops me off on his way to get Lucas), he tells me the street he lives on is two and a half miles long. I figure I'll run it once. Two or three miles was my usual distance when I exercised more frequently and cared more about my own health (before my first marriage and, especially, right after my divorce).

I don't have any good shirts to wear, so after I lace up my shoes, I take off down the street in my shorts and sports bra. The street is isolated, not that I care too much about my attire anyway. As I begin to run, I flip through some playlists on my phone and find one full of metal music.

By the time I hit the two-and-a-half-mile mark, I'm in the middle of Metallica's "Battery." I'm feeling amped up, so I turn back and run the opposite way. At the five-mile mark, I'm into Nine Inch Nails' "We're In This Together." *Well, I can't stop now.* After seven miles, I force myself to stop. Even though I'm exhausted, I know I could have kept going. I *would* have kept going. I knew what I was actually doing, though.

I was slapping myself all over again.

Self-punishment for living when someone I love is so close to not having that luxury.

I walk the last half mile back to Steve's place without listening to any music. I want to cry, but I am devoid of all fluid, because of my tears early this morning and my intense run this afternoon. So instead of crying, I walk like a zombie in an emotionless void.

Knowing the house is empty, I throw off my clothes the moment I step in the door, heading straight to the bathroom. I step into the shower before I even turn it on. No one, to my knowledge, does this, but I want the extreme cold or heat from the burst of water to snap me back into reality.

It doesn't work.

22

After adhering to our own mental health needs for a few hours, Steve and I return to the hospital. When we arrive, Dad is still there. Not only that, but he already has his pajamas and toothbrush laid out for his night's stay. We don't even discuss who will stay tonight, but I'm okay with him taking initiative, and I know Steve is, too.

It is always so silent when we enter the room, which adds a sense of dread when we look at our mother. It seems nothing has changed since this morning – or during the past four days – and I find that very confusing. How could she have been so close to death this morning, and yet still be here now, looking exactly the same? As if that living nightmare of a morning didn't actually happen?

I do not want Mom to die. I feel badly even looking for signs of further deterioration, because that's the last thing I want. But I also want her pain to end. Because she can't speak, it's impossible for any of us to determine her current level of pain. It's the most confusing, frustrating, exhausting, and soul-draining experience of my life.

Do I wish for her to be without pain, or do I wish for her to stay a little longer?

I honestly don't know.

"What did you kids do this afternoon?" Dad seems to be in a pleasant mood, despite the day's rough start.

"I got to visit Lucas," Steve says.

"Oh, good. What about you, Emma?"

"I exercised. Went for a run. A long one."

"Exercise is great for your mental health," Dad says.

Not when you're trying to "accidentally" kill yourself in the process, I think.

"I figured it was better than vegging out in front of the TV," I fabricate.

Dad sighs. "TV doesn't interest me anymore. There's no joy in it. Unless I'm with you guys."

"I know what you mean," Steve says. "I can't read a book or even take a drive without constantly thinking about what's going on in this room or if I'm missing out on something important."

"Your mom would want you to be happy," Dad reminds us. "You must remember that."

"I just want you guys to be okay."

"I know," Steve agrees. "It's just so difficult."

We all look at her. She is motionless. Her head faces the door. I can still hear her breathing, more softly than before, but just as labored. Her eyes seem more distant, and the film covering them is becoming thicker, because of her inability to blink. The nurses have done a good job of giving her baths, but they don't fashion her hair in any way, so her entire appearance looks off. She looks like she accidentally fell asleep in the middle of the day and was rushed out the door before she had a chance to "do anything" with herself – which she always did. She was always so concerned with her appearance – not in a vain way, but she always wanted to look her nicest. That's why, as her illness progressed, she still dressed up on Sundays, despite being unable to go to church. She'd hate the way she looks now, I know that for a fact.

Even so, I feel as though I am seeing her real strength and beauty for the first time. Here she is – on the final step between this world and the next – and she won't give in. It just adds to the legacy of her incredible stubbornness, which is also a trait I inherited and carry with pride. She will not go until she is ready, that much is clear. But when I look at her, I don't necessarily feel sorry for her. Sure, I wish she were in any other condition, but "Wish in one hand and shit in the other" as Dad used to say. "See which one fills up first."

But that's not the scenario we are dealing with.

My mother's situation is indeed dire, and yet she still holds strong. Despite her unbrushed hair, she looks great, at least to me, and I know Steve and Dad would agree. I have never known a stronger person than my mom, and I know I never will. Who else could let her blood pressure drop so low, hear all of her family say "goodbye," and still be like, "Nah, I don't think I'm quite ready yet"?

She is a remarkable woman. I hope I can be like her one day.

"So, what do you want to do tonight?" Steve snaps me out of another of my existential crises concerning the rest of my life.

"Given how rough this morning was," Dad says, "I thought we could do something nice for Annie. We could play some of her favorite songs, tell stories, and just... give her our love."

"Sounds good." I push down my instinct to immediately sob.

Dad, Steve, and I all take turns playing songs for Mom while we eat dinner and chat. Dad, of course, plays Pink Floyd. I don't even remember Mom being that big of a fan of the Floyd, but she and Dad lived a life before Steve and I came along, so who's to say?

Steve plays Mom some inspirational and Christian music that make the room feel like a revival and funeral service at the same time.

When I think about the times I spent as a kid with Mom in the car, I always remember her playing old '50s and '60s music. Stuff like early Marvin Gaye, The Drifters, The Turtles, Simon and Garfunkel, and The Four Tops. She wasn't as big of a fan of "hippies" like The Beatles, The Stones, or The Who, so I avoid playing them. But this also adds to my confusion about Dad's insistence that she listened to prog rock. Was she actually a secret hippy but just didn't want us to know?

After we eat and play one of the most eclectic playlists I can imagine, we take turns telling our favorite "Mom stories." Dad reminisces again about how they first met (I can't decide if he re-tells the story because it is his favorite or because his mind is slipping and he can't remember telling us the story already). He also tells a rather unique story that Steve and I have never heard.

Apparently, when Mom and he were dating, one of Mom's former suitors was having a tough time getting over her, even though she had clearly moved on. So, he began stalking her. When Dad was at Mom's apartment one night, they heard a vehicle honking outside. After looking out the window, they saw a truck speed off. The truck, of course, belonged to the former boyfriend. So, after two weeks of watching this nonsense on a nearly daily basis, Dad had enough. He waited outside on the porch one night while Mom watched from above, through the small window at the front of her apartment. To any passersby on the street, it would seem as though my Mom and Dad were both upstairs like any other night. When the guy with attachment issues showed up that night and parked his truck in the street, however, Dad silently walked up to his truck with a baseball bat. He smashed the truck's rear light before he made his way up to the driver's side mirror. After Dad connected and knocked it completely off, he stuck the bat the in the man's face. The dude was already freaking out, but having a bat placed squarely in his face sent the message, loud and clear, that Dad would take no more of this guy's shit. The guy pleaded for Dad to stop, and he agreed he would – after he jabbed him right in the nose with the fat end of the bat. With blood pouring down his face, the man began to cry out "Why?" His reply? "Well, you told Annie you'd leave her alone. How does it feel to be lied to?"

Steve and I burst into laughter. I find that I have newfound respect for him as well. The fact that he so passionately defended our mom is heartwarming to hear – even if it did end in an assault. Luckily, the ex never reported the incident. I can't be sure, but I think Dad made some additional threats to make sure it wasn't. After all, he dealt with militant communists, carnivorous beasts, and pistol-packing drug dealers. He wasn't afraid of some townie douchebag.

Next up, Steve tells his favorite story (that didn't involve the "Circumciser"). Steve reminds us about our trip to the Six Flags theme park in St. Louis. Mom hated roller coasters while Dad loved them. Likewise, Steve hated them, and I loved them. So, while Dad and I rode all of the big coasters over and over (the "Batman" was my favorite), Steve laughs about how he and Mom rode a small roller coaster called the "Caterpillar." Steve was probably ten years old at the time, and this coaster, if you can even call it that, was meant mostly for four-and five-year-olds. This *intense* ride comprised of one big loop with one rise and a drop in the middle. Although Steve swears the drop was enough to blow his hair back, I remember it being only a seven-foot drop *at most*. And I would remember. I laughed at him for being scared of it when we were kids, and I often brought it up over the years to show how much tougher I was than he, despite his older age.

  When it is my turn for a story, I struggle at first to decide upon one. I have so many great stories that I recall fondly. As the youngest member of the family, I feel as though I spent the most time with her, and yet, when I am put on the spot, I cannot decide upon a great story. I can't think of a laugh-filled, entertaining yarn involving an assault or rollercoasters, but I do think of one that means a lot to me.

  "I remember being in second grade," I begin, "and we were having our Valentine's Day party. I remember this party in particular because I left behind the Valentine box that we made at home, so I was the only kid in class without one. The teacher, doing the best she could on the spot, gave me a brown paper bag in its place. So, I decorated it with hearts and wrote 'Emma' on it, in big goofy letters, and colored them in with my best crayons (the best commodity a kid has at that age). Despite my efforts to 'pretty' it up, I was so embarrassed about my paper bag, and the other students quickly took notice. Behind the teacher's back, they made fun of my 'sack lunch' and refused to put Valentines in it. I felt so sick to my stomach that I thought about going to the school nurse to insist I go home. Right as I was about to ask permission to leave, however, in comes Mom – holding my Valentine's box. Immediately, my anxieties eased, and I ran to her. She bent down to hug me, and I thanked her over and over again in her ear. She put me at arm's length and said, 'You don't have to thank me. This is what parents do – pick up the slack for their forgetful children.' She was joking, of course, but there was a lot of truth in that, too. That's exactly what parents do, or *should* do. Mom was always there for me. She always looked out for me. She knew what was best for me, even if I disagreed at the time. She was the greatest." I pause after reflecting upon my last sentence. "She *is* the greatest."

As I lean down to hug her, I notice my father's eyes welling up. My story strikes a huge chord with him. Sure, he was there for most of our childhood vacations and holidays, but he was rarely there for our school parties, concerts, games, or art shows. He missed out on a lot of our childhood, and, therefore, he missed out on a lot of his life's happiness.

When I return to my seat, I look around the room. We all feel melancholy, yet we still put happy faces on. We are so happy that she is a part of our lives, even if we took days, weeks, months, or even years of that time for granted.

But that's life, isn't it? You never realize what's most important until it's too late.

After telling our parents goodbye, Steve and I head to his car. We spend most of the ride home in a comfortable silence. It's been a long day, and we're both exhausted. When we pull into his driveway, he finally speaks.

"You're a good sister, you know that?" And then, after a beat, he says, "And you're a great daughter."

Feeling incredibly uncomfortable with this show of sibling love (even though I share his sentiments), I manage a sincere smile. "You are too, Steve." I pause for emphasis and then add, "You're a great sister."

Steve pushes me into the car door on my side as we both erupt in laughter. "Can't you just be serious for one second and accept the fact that I am trying to express myself in a *positive* way? Do you even know what being positive means?"

"I'm sorry." I smile, but it turns into a head shake. "It's just... all too much."

"I know," he agrees forlornly. "Listen, I know it's been a long day, but do you wanna hang out for a bit?"

"And do what? Like drink or do drugs?"

"No, stupid. Let's just go hang out on my porch. Talk about stuff other than life and death for a while."

I search his eyes for truthfulness, and I can tell he is being honest. "Okay, but only if you have bug spray."

For the next two hours, after, perhaps, the longest day of our lives, Steve and I sit on his porch and chat the night away. We talk about our former exploits (which we have *still* kept hidden from our parents), our plans for the future, and some stories from the past that are enhanced with a darker sense of humor that would not be acceptable in front of our father. It is a perfect way to end the worst day of our lives.

And I figure we needed it, because, as we learned today, you never know what could happen in a matter of hours.

23

"Morning, Dad."

As we enter Mom's room, Dad is tidying up his chair-bed. Steve side-steps me to hand Dad a tall coffee. "How'd she do overnight?"

"Doesn't seem to be any change," he shrugs.

I am, of course, not disappointed by his answer. I'm just... confused.

How is it that her condition is changing less while under hospice care than it was when she was upstairs in an ordinary hospital room?

Seeming to pick up on what I'm thinking, Dad adds, "Doesn't make sense to me either."

"Hey, Mom." Steve leans over to kiss her. "Em and I just got here. Glad to see you again."

Mom stares out the window as she always does – unmoving and unresponsive. This horrific image of the woman who gave birth to me is unfortunately now the predominant image I have when I think of her.

There is a knock at the door, followed by slow footsteps. "Morning, Morrises," Nurse Geoffrey says. Steve and I smile when we see our favorite nurse again. Even Dad seems to smirk – just a tad. "How's Miss Annie this morning?"

"Like I was just telling them," Dad says, "she seems to have stayed pretty consistent since yesterday."

Geoffrey nods his head, brow furrowed. He looks at her mottled hands. "Okay, well it's that time of day when we would like to turn her over, if that is okay with you. Of course, there is always a risk of altering her breathing by doing so, but it does help with her comfort. It's totally up to you, though, whether you want to go ahead and keep her on this regular rotation."

The three of us exchange quick glances, once again, like Tuco, Blondie, and Angel Eyes in *The Good, the Bad, and the Ugly*. Without saying a word, we know we all agree.

"Let's go ahead," Dad says. "We want her to be comfortable."

"Okay," Geoffrey nods empathetically. "I'll call in my helper nurses, and we'll get it done. If you want…"

We already know the routine. "We'll be in the lobby," Dad mutters.

As the helpers enter, we depart, and as the door closes slowly behind us, I catch a glimpse of Mom as the nurses prepare to move her. Her eyes stay on the window – maybe the sky.

While we walk to the lobby, we know that nothing has *changed* compared to any other day. Mom's condition is stable. The usual nurses are on duty. The halls are still quiet.

A lot of the same faces look back from the rooms with open doors. Some faces have disappeared, replaced with new, frightened ones or freshly made beds. Of the faces that remain, nothing has changed for them either. The same disinterested adult children look down at their phones while their dying loved ones look up at the ceiling, praying for death. And, worst of all, the faces that were alone before are still alone. They face the unknown with no one to help ease their fear.

I hate this place. Nothing changes.

That being said, this walk feels different.

"We've got her turned and settled in," Geoffrey says, finding us silent – for once – in the lobby. "Her breathing has slowed a bit. That doesn't necessarily mean anything – *but it could.* I'd suggest going back to the room now, just in case." While it may sound like his words are worrisome, they don't come across that way. He delivers them calmly and reassuringly.

We follow him back to the room and find the other two nurses still there, monitoring Mom's condition. When we enter, though, they finish and quietly exit. "We'll be right outside your door," Geoffrey says. "If you feel like something has changed, or if you need anything at all, don't hesitate to push that button or holler for me."

"Thank you," I say. He gives a nod before leaving.

Dad, Steve, and I circle around Mom. She stares at the ceiling now, still unmoving and unresponsive. Her soft breathing rattles like a struggling daytime snore. No physical evidence suggests that she is more comfortable, but I feel as though she is. She *feels* more at ease. Or maybe that is just what I want to believe.

And then it happens for the first time – she stops breathing.

24

It takes a moment for us to register that Mom's raspy breathing has ceased, but we suddenly all pick up on it.

"Do you...?" Steve begins.

"Yeah..." I add.

Dad leans over to inspect her. He tilts his head to the side to try to hear a breath. He shakes his head. "I don't hear anything."

"Should we...?"

Before I can finish my question, Steve is out the door, grabbing Geoffrey. They rush in, and Dad backs away so Geoffrey can have a turn inspecting her.

And then – she takes a breath. She sounds like a fish gasping for air on dry land.

A wave of anxious relief washes over our family. "Do you have an idea of how long she went without a breath?"

"About twenty seconds," Steve says.

Of course, he was counting, I think. *He's so on top of everything.*

"What does that mean?" Dad says.

"This is pretty common for the end of life," Geoffrey says solemnly. "If I were to take a guess... I think today will probably be the day."

I begin to softly cry at yet another reality check. I spent so much of the past year in denial, and now I have no chance to take a breath myself.

Then it happens again. She stops breathing.

Geoffrey leans over, eyes on his watch, counting. We all unconsciously hold our breath as well, both in anxiousness at the situation and, perhaps, feeling undeserving of air ourselves until she can take another one.

She stares at the ceiling, mouth slightly open. She is completely silent, and her eyes are frozen. If not for Geoffrey's calmness, I would have already assumed she passed away. And then, just like before, she gasps for air. It almost sounds painful.

"About twenty-five seconds," Geoffrey says, lowering his wrist. "I'd say you were about spot-on, Steve."

"How long is she going to keep doing this?" I ask.

Geoffrey slowly turns toward me. "Until the end."

For the next fifteen minutes, I watch my Mom die a dozen times. Each time she goes without a breath, it truly feels like it is her last moment. It's the most painful experience of my life, and I cannot escape it.

Suddenly, during an especially long stretch without a breath (probably close to forty seconds), Geoffrey steps away and quietly calls in the other two nurses. They promptly enter and man their stations.

"What's going on?" Dad asks.

"Her breathing has slowed dramatically," Geoffrey says. "I think these might be her final moments."

As Mom continues to stare at the ceiling, unblinking and unmoving, we begin to silently cry, but we hold back the true force of our sorrows for her sake. Dad plants himself in the chair, in shock, but continues to hold her hand. He softly whispers her name.

Steve sits in front of me. He grabs her other hand.

I sit behind him and grab a hold of her ankle.

The two other nurses slightly back away as Geoffrey monitors her pulse.

While I hate the sudden sound of her gasp of air, I want nothing more than to be jolted by it now. I want to hear her breathe one more time, just so I can tell her that I love her one more time and hope that she is conscious enough to hear me.

Just one more time.

Geoffrey slowly places Mom's hand back and looks at the clock.

"Time of death for Annie Morris is 10:40 a.m., June 17th."

25

I burst into a sob and bury my face in my brother's back. Dad wails a high-pitched cry that I've never heard, or want to hear, again. Steve, surprisingly, stays strong – most likely for Dad and me as our grief overtakes us. Despite his incredible strength, though, I notice Steve's shoulders jerk in sync with his silent tears.

"I'm so sorry," Geoffrey says. The other two nurses have their heads bowed.

"Thank you," Dad says. I'm surprised to hear him speak first, supplanting Steve. "Thank you for all you did for her – and us."

Geoffrey nods appreciatively and says something about a coroner, a gurney, and something else, but I cannot decipher his words or how they relate to each other. It all sounds like mush.

While Dad and Steve listen intently to Geoffrey's instructions on what to do next, I find myself outside my body witnessing this event. I see myself looking at Mom. We both appear lifeless, but unfortunately only the wrong one is.

I stare at her mouth that no longer produces air. I stare at the eyes that no longer see me. I stare at the heart that no longer loves us.

I finally lift my hand from her lifeless body and feel the warmth of the air in the room. My hand has grown accustomed to the coldness of her skin, so everything else seems unnatural.

"Em." Steve slightly jostles my shoulder.

"Yeah?" I mutter, trying to return to my physical body.

"Come on, let's go. The coroner is arriving soon. They said we probably don't want to be here for that."

"What about Dad?"

Steve looks over at our remaining parent. "He's staying with her."

When we get to the hospital's main lower level waiting area, we find Mallory and Lucas already there waiting. Lucas immediately runs to Steve as he falls to his knees to be at his son's level. Lucas is so young and small compared to his father, yet he seems to be effectively consoling his daddy. Their roles are reversed, just as mine and Steve's with Dad were for the past week or so.

Steve pulls away from Lucas and holds him at arm's length. Lucas wipes his tears with his small arm. "Gramma's in heaven?"

A look of pain, unlike any I've ever seen on anyone, crosses my brother's face. He brushes Lucas's hair back a couple of times until he finds the strength to answer. "Yeah," he exhales in a soft cry. "Grandma's in heaven now."

Lucas starts to cry harder. "But I don't want her to go away."

Steve attempts to smile, finding his fatherly shoes again. "I don't either, Buster. I don't either. But you know what? She's happier now, because she doesn't hurt anymore.

And she doesn't have to stay in this old, gross hospital anymore either."

Lucas nods slowly. Steve pulls him in for a hug that seems to last forever. Steve kisses the top of his son's head before standing and stepping over toward Mallory, who has situated herself about six feet back to give her ex privacy with their son.

"Hey, Mal. Thanks for bringing him."

Mallory grabs Steve and hugs him. It's not a rekindled romance sort of hug. Instead, it's a hug representing sorrow for someone she once cared for. "I'm so sorry, Steve." She gently rubs his back as he places his face into her shoulder. Clearly, he is trying to avoid crying in front of her. Why he cares, I do not know, but at the same time, I kind of get it. "She was a tough lady."

"The toughest," Steve chuckles through a sob. He finally releases Mallory and steps back.

"She got diagnosed when she was already at stage four, right?"

"That's right."

Mallory shakes her head. "And she still fought so long. Over a year. That's incredible."

"It really is." Steve then beckons his son over. He says to him, "Go give your aunt Em a hug. She could really use one."

Lucas sets his sights on me as I crouch down and engulf him. "I love you, Emmie," he says in my ear.

I squeeze him harder. "I love you, Lukie."

"I miss Gramma," he says when I look at his devastated face.

My bottom lip turns downward instantly. "I do too. I miss her already."

PART THREE

Grief

26

I find myself in a funeral home.

I'm not exactly sure how I got here. I don't know who drove me here. It's possible I even drove myself, which is a scary thought. Much like when I first saw Mom's deceased body before me, I feel out of sync with my body. I don't want to be here. At all.

But that's life for us – the living.

"Have you thought much about the vessel in which you want to place her body?" the funeral home director asks. His name is Gary Underwood, and he knows Dad professionally – I guess that's what you would call it – from Dad's years of researching "death and grieving" for his documentaries. In my opinion, I would rather go anywhere other than a funeral home named "Six Feet Underwood," but that's just me. I don't get to make those decisions.

He does seem to have a nice business card, though. While he and Dad re-acquaint themselves, I turn the card over. I evaluate Gary's office like those businessmen in *American Psycho*. On the back of his off-white, fairly sturdy card, it simply says, "Call Gary if it's time to bury!"

"I think we were thinking an urn," Dad says, once again taking the lead from Steve. Actually, it's not so much that he's taking anything *away* from Steve, it's just that Steve appears shell-shocked and unable to be at the top of his game.

"We were?" I ask Dad. "I didn't think…"

"That's what your mom requested," Dad shrugs. Based on his body language, I can tell he's not happy with her decision either. His hands are tied to Mom's final wishes, however. He doesn't get to make those decisions.

Gary spies Dad shifting uncomfortably in his seat. "Is everything ok?"

"It's just," Dad grumbles, "seats are kinda stiff."

"People don't usually sit long enough to break them in, I suppose."

"Are the seats in the chapel area the same make?"

"They are."

"This is going to be a nightmare," Dad says under his breath.

"Well, um…" Mr. Underwood redirects, "we have a great selection of urns downstairs. Would you like to see them now? We can address any need."

What kinds of needs do we have left?

"Needs?" Dad says, reading my mind.

"Well, you know, depending upon how you, or your religion or philosophy, feel about the matter."

"Explain."

"Well, we have metal, veneer, fiberglass, hardwood, and even eco-friendly, if you're so inclined."

"I'm not."

"Okay, sure. No problem"

"Actually," Dad rethinks, "go ahead and give me the deets. You've got me all curious."

"The eco-friendly vessels can be made from cardboard, seagrass, willow, or even bamboo. And none of the materials will harm the environment!"

"Well, that is good to hear. My primary concern is to *not* harm the environment in the process of placing my wife under a mound of dirt."

"I-I'm sorry. I didn't mean…"

"Dad, stop it," I interrupt. "Dad's a natural born antagonist. He's just being difficult. Trying to make you uncomfortable."

"It's workin'," Gary mutters.

"I can speak for myself. Think I won't?"

"We all know you're more than capable…"

Shifting on his feet, perhaps realizing there is a side of Dad he didn't know, Gary pivots the subject back to urns. "Would you like to go take a look?"

Edges of caskets stick out of the walls like prized game trophies. They're polished and shiny, with only subtle differences to make the decision-making even more difficult. On the "show room floor," full-sized caskets are on display. There is one reasonably priced coffin in the front of the room, but like a car dealership, the prices only increase the further we walk.

I find myself looking inside the caskets as we walk past them. I don't picture Mom lying inside of them, as one might imagine. Instead, I see myself in each casket. I am at peace, finally rested, and free from stress. It sounds morbid, but I almost envy the imaginary dead version of myself, with my hands crossed over my chest like a dormant vampire.

That Emma doesn't have to worry any more. She doesn't have to lose anyone else.

As I imagine myself inside each coffin, I look at Dad, who is basically kicking the tires of each casket he comes across. To him, they are race horses. He evaluates each one, determining which one would "win the race" of preserving the deceased body best, I suppose.

Steve, on the other hand, just stares forward, totally zoned out. I'm not sure what stage of grief he is currently in, but it's by far the most distant and least interactive one.

"Where are the urns?" Dad asks after inspecting the final, and most expensive coffin, almost grumpily.

"If you take a left turn around the back of the room, you'll see them displayed there," Gary says.

We make the turn and find the urns. They are all lined up and displayed like World Series trophies. A few stand out as vastly different from the others, but most of them are basically the same – just different colors and textures.

"We have all shapes and sizes here at Six Feet Underwood. Everything from traditional models to modern molds. Our selection runs from blue, black, or red in a spherical chalice to neon, pink, and tie-dye in an urn shaped like a hippie Buddha."

"That's redundant," Dad says.

"Of course, if you want a 'character' urn," Mr. Underwood continues, "we'll have to ship that in."

"How about a sparkling ruby red one modeled after Mammy from *Gone with the Wind*?" Dad remarks.

"I can certainly check our online catalogue!"

"He's just giving you a hard time," I say.

"How about I go wait upstairs while you give them a look over?" Gary says, backing away.

Once he's out of earshot, and I know I can have a *real* conversation, I ask Dad, "How about a plain black urn? Simple, not flashy. Shows respect without really trying too hard."

"Seems kinda plain, though. Like I just picked the first one that was offered. Shows a lack of caring."

I silently evaluate the selection a bit longer. "Do you know Mom's favorite color?"

"Blue."

I begin scouring the display for all of the blue choices. I find one at the top and point it out. "What about that one?"

He scoffs.

"What?"

"Eh, I dunno…".

"What don't you know? It's a nice blue… it's sleek and elegant. Very feminine."

"It just seems a little too… *sexy*."

"Sexy?! What do you mean? It's an urn, Dad."

He tilts his head to the side. "Am I wrong? It's kind of glittery… very shapely…"

"Dad."

"… especially around the *bottom*…"

"*Dad*!"

"What?"

"Would you prefer a thinner, sleeker version then?"

"Em, we're talking about your mother here."

"What, Mom wasn't thin and sleek in her day?"

"Of course she was. I just don't think it's very respectable is all."

"Okay, well which one of these do you see as 'respectable'?"

Dad evaluates them and then confidently says, "That one." He points at one toward the bottom. It also happens to be one of the cheapest.

"*That* one?"

"What's wrong with that one?"

"It's black. It looks bland. Like a matte photo."

"Urns aren't Cadillacs, Em. You don't need to go with the fully loaded option to show how much you loved someone."

I take his point and try to find another "respectable" option. "What about that one?"

Dad looks at the urn in the middle I point out. His face drops. "No," he says simply.

"Why not? It's more traditional and basic. It's a tasteful design, no *flashy curves*, a nice color…"

"It's brown."

"Well, it's a light brown. It looks very nice."

"Brown."

"What's wrong with brown."

Dad's eyes well up. "Brown – like the dirt she's going to be covered up with in just a couple of days. You wouldn't even know she was there."

I fall as silent as Steve, which makes me look at him. Steve finally looks up, sensing the change in emotion in Dad. "I didn't know we'd still bury her…" I mutter.

Dad exhales. "I don't know what to do. Annie said she didn't want to be put up on a shelf for display for 'dinner party guests.'" He pauses and adds, "But I have a hard time thinking about her being that far away. Underground…"

A tear falls from his eye and he promptly turns away and grabs a brochure, which he is clearly not reading. I attempt to put a hand on his back, but he senses me and steps toward the exit.

"Let's go with 'Baby Blue' up there."

"Dad?" The room is dead silent when I address him. "If you had your choice, how would you like to handle her final resting place?"

Without any hesitation, he says, "I would get a casket. I don't want…"

Although he never says the words, I know what he is thinking. *I don't want her to burn…* I cannot help but think the same thing.

"Then let's do that."

"It's not what she…"

"It is, though. She wanted what was best for us. What would make us less sad. And I think," I glance over at Steve, who gives me a slight head nod, "I speak for all of us when I say that will make all of us less sad. And we need all the help we can get right now."

We softly ascend the stairs to the main level of the funeral home. I don't know why we are sneaking the way we are, but it is instinctive.

"Hey there!" Gary Underwood surprises us as we turn a corner. This greeting nearly garners him another three casket sales. "Were you able to find a satisfactory vessel?"

Why does he keep calling it a "vessel"? Makes it sound like the Starship Enterprise or something.

"Yeah, we're going with a casket after all," Dad says. He hands over the brochure and points, "This one."

Knowing his selections well, Gary nods and says, "That's a very nice choice, Jim."

"What else do we need to accomplish here, Gary?"

"Well, you'll want to go to a flower shop and pick out an arrangement, I suppose. You can also decide if you'd like us to make a slideshow for the funeral. Find a pastor for the service. And..." his words slow down, knowing the next thing he has to say can be painful to hear, "We can arrange a viewing of the body. It can be a large visitation for the community, or just a small gathering for family or whoever you'd like. It's up to you. Is that something you'd like to consider?"

"Yes," Steve says, finally offering an opinion on something, anything. "I want to see her again."

27

We drive to a local flower shop, and the leftover feelings from Six Feet Underwood spill over.

"I've never seen a more complicated purchase in my life," I say, sitting shotgun.

As Dad navigates the road, it's clear he thinks he is navigating the problems of the world with as much ease. "You've got to keep them guessing, kids. Otherwise they will corner you into their idea of the 'best fit,' which is often the best fit for their wallet."

"I thought you were friends with Mr. Underwood?"

"I am. But Gary has to earn a living just like everyone else."

I sigh. "You might be the most cynical person I've ever known."

"I'm not a cynic. I'm a realist."

We pull into the parking lot of the flower shop, just a few blocks away from the funeral home in Hudson. Once we reach the counter, we are offered condolences again. Dad is pretty well-known in this area, despite his reclusiveness, because of his films, so word of his wife's death spread pretty quickly.

"So sorry to hear about Annie," the female clerk, bordering on a buck-twenty in age, says. "She was so beautiful, inside and out."

"Thanks," Dad says, head down. "We need to pick out a flower arrangement."

"Of course," she says, bending down, with great effort, below the counter. I stand on my tippy toes when it appears as though she disappears after more than a few silent seconds. *Either she broke a hip or she ducked for cover.* I figure that any time she gets that low down, it's just ingrained in her to get underneath the desk. Those nuclear bomb drills really got pounded into the "Greatest Generation's" heads. On my toes, I see her ankle-length dress wriggle, though, and I know she is alive and coming back up for air. When she gets back up, she drops a large catalogue with an audible thud. "Take a look through this," she says, "and I'll be back in a few minutes."

As she disappears into the backroom, I begin flipping the pages as Dad looks over my shoulder. Essentially, all of the arrangements look the same to me. I'm not super "girly girly," if that makes sense, or is even still acceptable to say. But, hey, I'm a woman, so I can say whatever I want about myself. I like what I like, and I've never cared for plant life. They all look the same to me, and the idea of trying to keep a plant alive fills me with more anxiety – which I certainly do not need. Plus, each time a leaf falls, in its brown and decayed state, I feel a great sense of guilt. This living *thing* is just deteriorating in front of me, begging for me to save it, and my only solution is to say "Sorry" as I drown it in water.

"Do you know what Mom's favorite flower was? Maybe that will make this easier."

Dad thinks for a moment. "I don't really know things like that. She liked those yellow ones, but I don't know what they were called. I didn't buy her many plants over the years. She could never keep them alive."

So that's where I get my inability to keep something healthy and alive.

"Lilacs," Steve says from behind us. "She liked lilacs."

I nod. "Well, let's find some yellow lilacs then."

The flower shop trip is a short one, but I have a feeling our next stop will not be.

"Time to visit the pastor?" I ask.

Dad grunts.

"What's his name again?"

"Father Jacobs."

"I don't think he's a 'Father.' He's not Catholic."

"Fine, it's Reverend Jacobs or Brother Jacobs or Family Friend Jacobs. You know what I mean. His last name is Jacobs."

"Why the hostility toward a man of the cloth?" I ask with a smirk.

"It's not because he's a 'man of the cloth,'" Dad mocks. "It's because he's younger than either of you two. How is someone that young supposed to handle something like this? A ceremony for Annie?"

"Let's go find out."

28

Dad, Steve, and I step out of the car that we parked right in front of Hudson's one and only Baptist church. It's intimidating to look at, but I'm not sure why. It's not because I'm an atheist or anything. I think it might be because I have been made so angry by this whole death process, and I have had no one to blame... other than God. I know people die every day. I know I'm not unique in that regard. *I know all of that.* But I cannot help but feel, in my heart, that this is a personal attack, even though, in my brain, I know that notion is ridiculous.

The day is getting late. We have been going non-stop all day. It feels as though Mom died a week ago, not yesterday. And yet sometimes it feels like she died an hour ago. Or that it didn't even happen. Time is slowly becoming irrelevant as we prepare to say goodbye to the matriarch of our family. The setting sun is just visual representation of that idea, I suppose.

"Let's get this over with," Dad says reluctantly.

As soon as we get to the steps of the church, Pastor Jacobs emerges. "Welcome, Morris family," he says in a voice that actually feels empathetic and not put-on. "Please come in."

We follow him inside. Dad grunts again.

"*Annie* was a regular at church, so I got to know her well during my time here," Pastor Jacobs says after we find seats in different church pews. I can't help but feel like the way that he says Mom's name is meant to impart guilt upon the rest of us. Or maybe that guilt is just living within me.

"You've had a pretty short tenure here so far, right?" Dad asks, clearly poking fun at his age.

"Short, yes, but fruitful," Jacobs says, brushing off the comment. "Enough time to hear the legend and lore of you, Mr. Morris."

Dad grunts.

The pastor turns to Steve and me. "I only provoke him because he enjoys it. Everyone else seems too afraid of him," he says with a wink.

"Maybe they're onto something," Dad snarls.

"How long have I tried to get you to come here?"

"I think I receive a call or postcard from you about every month…"

"Ever since I met Annie."

"Dad was never the church-going type," I admit.

"Every person can be the 'church-going type.' It just takes some conviction." Pastor Jacobs smiles to himself. "Truly, I love this town and the people in it – Annie included. She was a special lady."

Dad nods his head. I gaze around looking at the church décor. Steve sits behind us, staring at the floor.

Yes, the pastor is young, but Jacobs is clearly well-trained in handling death and grieving families. He promptly picks up the conversation again and steers it in the direction it needs to go. "I want to make this as simple as possible for you guys. I know Annie wouldn't have wanted to make a big fuss over everything. What would you like from me?" he asks. "How do you envision the service?"

"See, Dad?" I say. "Not everyone is trying to up-sale you."

"'Up-sale'?" the pastor asks, somewhat aghast.

"Dad was just educating us on his pessimistic..."

"Realistic," Dad interjects.

"...view of people earlier," I finish.

"Well I can assure you that there is no pessimism or *up-selling* to be found here. Everyone in the congregation loved Annie. And that's why I want to get her service right. So what can I do to help you along in this?"

Dad winces, presumably because he actually does envision the service in his head, so I tap in for him. "Well, what's a 'normal' funeral service usually look like?"

"The guests are seated first. Usually a song plays while they enter, either a song you've chosen or we can have our church pianist play hymns. After that, the family is seated at the front. I will then read a short scripture from the Bible and then a brief eulogy – the one that was printed in the local paper. After that, I can say a few words of personal remembrance if you'd like, or I can immediately hand it off to whoever wants to give their own eulogies. Once that's done, another song is usually played, followed by a prayer, and then you will be escorted out to the graveside, followed by the rest of the mourners who choose to come along."

"Okay, I think that all sounds *okay*..." I reply. "What do you think Dad? Steve?"

"No need to break the formula," Dad says.

I look back for Steve's thoughts and he simply nods his head, face still pointed downward.

"Okay, let's go with the usual then," Pastor Jacobs says. I know he doesn't mean to sound like a waiter at a Waffle House, but he kind of does. "Any idea on who would like to give a eulogy? No one *has* to, but one to three is pretty standard."

A heavy silence falls over us, which is only intensified by our surroundings in the big, empty sanctuary. There is something about a church's high ceiling that amplifies the smallness of man and how we never understand the full picture. Finally, Dad speaks up. "I can speak."

It may not seem like much – a husband giving a eulogy – but Dad's not a talker. He dislikes showing emotion or affection. Frankly, he dislikes people. So much so that he has secluded himself for years now. I'm honestly proud of him for being the first to step up. In fact, he inspires me.

"I can do one, too," I say softly. Dad looks at me, and gives me a small smile and nod.

Steve remains silent behind us.

"Sounds good," the pastor says. "So, the next thing… any ideas on songs you would like played?"

"Do they have to be… *religious* or…?" Dad begins.

"No, they don't *have* to be, although great comfort, for you and the other mourners, can be found in the traditional hymns or even modern songs."

Dad groans as he thinks. "Well, your mom was always a fan of the Floyd…"

"Not this again," I mutter.

"'The Floyd'?" Pastor Jacobs asks.

"Yeah," Dad continues. "Ya know, Pink Floyd? She loved *Dark Side* and *Wish You Were Here* the most."

"No, Dad," I say simply.

"What?" he scoffs.

"We are not cranking Pink Floyd at Mom's funeral."

"Why not? It's what she enjoyed. Shouldn't this be about what she enjoyed? A celebration of life and all..."

"Yes, but I don't want to turn her death into a laser rock show."

Dad rolls his eyes. Pastor Jacobs speaks up again. "Could I recommend something?"

"What's that?" I ask, desperate for anything other than stoner rock.

He leans forward. "I happen to know Annie's favorite hymn. She requested it often during services. It's called 'It Is Well.'"

"I'm not familiar with that one," Dad admits.

"I don't think you're familiar with anything connected to this building," I mumble.

Ignoring me, Pastor Jacobs gives us some backstory about Mom's favorite hymn.

"'It Is Well' was written by a man named Horatio Spafford. The Great Chicago fire of 1871 ruined him financially. Spafford was set to sail to Europe with his family before that terrible fire happened, but, instead, he had to stay back in the United States.

"A lot of complications arose with his business in Chicago after the fire. There was nothing he could do, but he still wanted his family to enjoy the trip as planned. So, in accordance with his wishes, his wife went ahead and took their four daughters on the boat to Europe.

"During the voyage, however, their ship collided with another ship in the middle of the Atlantic Ocean. Once she was able, Spafford's wife sent a telegram to her husband in Chicago that simply stated, 'Saved alone...'

"Spafford quickly got on a boat to meet his wife after he heard about the accident. He wrote the hymn 'It Is Well' as his ship passed over the spot where his four daughters had perished in the ocean below.

"In the midst of all that horrible despair, something wonderful was able to push its way up to the surface. Something beautiful.

"I think that's what drew Annie to the song."

"I guess that would work," Dad gives in, feeling guilty for not knowing the *current* version of his wife as well as this young man did.

"Tell you what," Jacobs adds. "'Shine On You Crazy Diamond' has a really long intro, doesn't it?"

"Yeah..." Dad says, perplexed.

"We could play that as people wait for the family to enter. Deal?"

"You know the Floyd?" Dad asks, with the edges of his mouth turning up just a bit.

Pastor Jacobs returns a smile. "'Every year is getting shorter...'"

"'...never seem to find the time,'" Dad finishes with a chuckle.

"Before I went to the seminary to become a pastor, I was a normal college student," Jacobs says.

Dad full-out laughs. The preacher man has officially won Dad's respect. "I never..." he trails off.

"What?" Pastor Jacobs eggs on.

Dad shakes his head. "I just never thought my opinion of you would change. No offense," he quickly adds. "You're just so young, I didn't think we could ever find common ground. Or that I would trust you with Annie's service," he says, words growing softer the more he talks. "But now, strangely enough, I know I can."

Pastor Jacobs smiles. Dad is a unique person, no doubt, but he is not the first to initially lack confidence in the young preacher. "The Lord works in mysterious ways," Pastor Jacobs smirks.

29

Dad drops Steve and me off before heading home. We offered to go home with him for the night, but he refused. I know he is lonely, but he does not want to appear weak in front of us. So, reluctantly, we agree to part for the night.

"See you in the morning," I say as Dad rolls up his window. He gives a wave and then drives off.

Steve is already on his porch by the time I say goodbye.

"I know this is a stupid question, but are you okay, Steve?"

He looks over his shoulder at me. "I'm fine, Em. Just tired. I'll see you in the morning, okay?" And then, remembering that he is my "host," he adds, "You need anything before I nod off?"

"No, I'm good." I feel sad watching my once-strong brother clearly falling apart. "Goodnight, Steve-o."

"Goodnight, Emmer."

I am almost asleep, holding Ezekiel firmly, when I hear a loud crack. It's more than a crack, though. It's a crack combined with a deep thud. And a primal scream.

It's Steve.

I have never been afraid of my brother in my life, but something tells me I should stay right where I am. I grip

Zeke even tighter as I hear my sibling continue to scream, curse, and, apparently, destroy his bedroom.

As I listen to my brother rage, I find myself not knowing what to do. I take a step toward the door to leave, to give him space, but then I step back again, knowing he might need my support when he finally calms down. As with every situation I've been thrown into this week, I simply do not know the right thing to do.

Steve's anger finally dissipates after about thirty minutes, and then I don't hear another sound. As softly as I can, I raise myself up from Lucas's toddler bed, crack open the door, and peer down the hallway toward his room. Steve's door is slightly ajar.

I walk on my tippy toes, as though I'm a decade younger sneaking out of my parents' house, until I reach his bedroom. I push his door open a bit wider, without a sound, so I can see what exactly has happened. Steve is passed out on his bed, lying on top of his covers, and still fully dressed. I step into his room to evaluate the damage.

His closet door, made of thick, solid oak, has a hole right through its center. Wood splinters down from the hole in a sharp V shape, and I see smears of blood all over the door. His dresser is all but destroyed. The drawers have all been pulled out and pulverized, with clothes strewn about. What was once a fine antique furniture set is now a starter pack for a fire pit. And in his wall, next to his bed, is an imprint of a fist. This is where I see the most blood. Steady streams trickle from it, contrasting sharply against the wall's white paint.

I look at my brother, lying face down on the bed. He is snoring loudly, almost violently. He is sleeping as heavily as I've seen anyone sleep. I gently grab his dominant hand to inspect it. All four knuckles are cut open – the middle two devastatingly so. They may even need stiches. I could be wrong – inspecting the wounds in the dark – but I swear I can see bone protruding through his middle knuckle. His fingers are cut up and are already massively swollen. I wouldn't be surprised if bones were fractured throughout his hand. One large gash across the top of his hand completes the gruesome image. It's a deep cut, and it appears to be the source of the most blood loss.

Why did you do this, Steve?

Why are my brother's instincts telling him to deal with his grief by acting out in anger and hurting himself?

In my own newly freshened grief, I find I am barely able to stand, let alone destroy an entire room like Orson Welles in *Citizen Kane* (I still don't like movies, but that scene was cemented in my brain, in an otherwise boring film, when Dad forced me to watch it as a child). It's especially weird given that Steve has always been the most level-headed member in our *entire* family. For him to act out this way is just bizarre. I feel like one of those dumbfounded neighbors on the news who didn't realize John Wayne Gacy had over thirty bodies buried under his house. "He was the last guy I would have expected…"

But those are probably the exact reasons Steve acted the way he did. After holding the family on his shoulders like that for years, including carrying Dad's lack of involvement early on, he finally just snapped.

Because he could not stop it from happening.

He could not save her life.

Three Days Later

30

The past few days have been a blur while we await Mom's visitation. All the plans for her funeral, and everything else, seem to be falling into place without much effort from Dad, Steve, or me, but I have to imagine that it's because we are working with professionals who do this on a weekly basis. While that should make me feel better, it does not. My mom has become just another statistic – the situation of the week for the funeral home, pastor, flower shop, and grave diggers. Everyone has a mother, but I'm still bitter about the fact that mine is just another number to everyone but my family.

In just a couple hours, though, this whole process will come to a close. Tonight is Mom's visitation. Tomorrow is her funeral. After that, the world moves on, and we will be left to deal with our grief on our own again.

I have been to a handful of visitations in my life, so I have a general idea of what I'm supposed to wear and how I am supposed to compose myself. I need to clothe myself entirely in black but somehow appear as though I am comfortable with the situation – which, for those who do not know, involves standing right next to my mother's lifeless body as a line of people come and give us their condolences after they view her.

Who started this morbid shit?

Whose great idea was it to invite all of our friends, neighbors, extended family, coworkers, and acquaintances to look at my dead mother right before trying to say something to us that is supposed to make us feel better?

And whose even greater idea was it to have us stand right next to her casket? Couldn't she at least be placed in another room? But then she would feel distant... *What would they say about her if we were* not *in earshot?*
I don't have the answers. I just don't like the questions.

To prepare for this delightful evening, I'm back at my living quarters, for the first time in a long time, to pick out the second-to-most-grim outfit I have (the most grim outfit will be saved for tomorrow, of course). After a couple hours of staring into my closet – mostly thinking about other things or nothing at all – I grab a black top, black leggings, and short, black, military-esque boots. After all, I feel as though I'm going into combat. I'll save my black dress for tomorrow.

After throwing everything on, I look at my disgusting appearance in my bathroom mirror. I do not know who looks more dead at this point. I'm so pale, devoid of fluid from my reddened tear ducts, and my nose is always on the verge of a nosebleed from constant sniffling. My hair is also a mess – Why should today be any different? – but I honestly don't care. And then I feel badly for thinking that.

You're saying goodbye to your mom... Can't you at least try for her?

With a huff, I brush out my hair. I cannot help but notice that more hair than usual seems to pull out within the bristles of my hairbrush. Then, I tie my hair back neatly with a black hairband. I put on some black mascara, but that is the only makeup I will adorn myself with. I don't want to look as though I'm using this horrendous event as a speed dating situation, nor do I have the strength to do a whole thing with my face.

Once I'm done, I take one last look. I barely recognize myself. My eyes appear lifeless, which perfectly matches my Grim Reaper appearance. I can't tell if I should be jacking myself into "The Matrix" or if I'm attending a barbaric death send-off. Unfortunately, I know it's the latter, because I don't know kung fu.

I ride with Steve to the funeral home in Hudson. It was out of my way to drive to his house first, but I really didn't want to go into that place by myself. Although his face is pretty much devoid of emotion, I know he is glad I came along with him.

Once we arrive, we park in the "family" section of the lot, which is right up front. Another great perk of being bereaved. We pull into a spot next to Dad's car. He's already gone inside, which means it is time for us to follow suit.

"You ready for this?" Steve turns off the car's engine.

"Not at all," I mutter. I feel like I'm having another out-of-body experience. Without so much as a thought, I instinctively grab my bottle of Xanax from my purse and pop one into my mouth. While I'm not feeling overwhelming anxiety right now, I know a wave will hit me as soon as we walk through those doors.

Steve watches me down a dry pill and furrows his brow. "You want some more time? We don't have to go in right now." He looks at the digital clock on his car's console.

"We got here about twenty minutes early, and the visitors won't arrive for close to ninety."

I take a deep breath. "No, I'm okay. I'm sure." I look over at the hand closest to me – his right one – and notice the swelling, cuts, and freshly made scabs. "Are you good, LaMotta?"

Steve barley glances down. He knows what I'm referring to. "Don't worry about me."

"Hate to remind you," I respond, "but we basically only have each other now."

"How are you dealing with it?" he pleads.

My eyes widen and I shrug. "I don't think I am at this point really."

Steve nods. "Eventually you will."

"Will you let me join your 'Fight Club' when I'm ready?"

"Em… the first rule of 'Fight Club'…"

"…is you don't talk about 'Fight Club.' Yeah, yeah, yeah," I finish his sentence. We both get a chuckle out of that. "Seriously, though… don't take your anger too far. Mom wouldn't want that."

At the mention of "Mom," Steve tenses up and puts his "I'm okay" mask back on. "Let's go," he says, opening his door.

31

If you have never experienced a funeral home's environment, you're lucky. Funeral homes all have a weird air about them, especially when one of your loved ones lies in one of the visiting rooms. They are structured like a normal house in many ways, but then they break off into different rooms that look like small church sanctuaries. And then, of course, there is a big selection of coffins and urns in the basement. No me gusta.

Steve and I slowly walk down the narrow hallway, which eerily feels like a hallway from the Overlook Hotel, until we hear muffled voices in a side room. It's our father and Mr. Underwood. Steve and I glance at each other and proceed.

Once we reach the voices, we notice the collage of pictures that has been prepared of our mother. It stands outside the visitation room's door. We take a moment to look over the familiar pictures, out of respect, but also because we want to push the inevitable as far off as we can.

The collage is probably twenty by thirty inches, and it sits on an easel. The pictures showcase her entire life – her as a child with her family, her as a teenager in high school and with friends, her and my father dating and then engaged, her during their early married life when it was still full of joy, her with miniature versions of Steve and myself and various household pets, and then her with the adult versions of us. As the years passed, fewer pictures were taken, and even fewer of her and Dad together were taken. In many ways, it's like her life ended years ago, back when Steve and I both left the house.

Without a word, Steve and I finish looking at her history at the same time, give each other a nod, and then step toward the doorway that leads the way to the woman in those pictures.

Steve and I slowly head toward the front of the room. Dad and Mr. Underwood are seated on the front pew. They chat quietly, but all I can focus on is... *her.*

There she is.

The woman who gave birth to me.

Raised me. Loved me.

And she's not moving.

In many ways, the past week has felt like a nightmare. It's been terrible, scary, and life-altering – but I still felt as though I could awaken from it when I am ready. It's only when I see the top of my mother's profile, sticking up from inside the casket, that I know I am not in control of this situation. I was in denial. Steve was right – eventually I will have to deal with this.

Steve and I stand together as we look down at her. Her casket is already surrounded by flowers that have been sent by loved ones and well-wishers, but she cannot appreciate them. I know she is still my mother, but she looks... *different.* In hospice care, I got so used to her sickly appearance that I accepted that as her "normal" look. Because she was at least still alive. Now, ironically, in death she looks more like the version of herself that was posted all over that collage.

Mom is wearing a nice burgundy sweater that I picked out for her, and her hair is brushed out and looks great. On her crossed hands, I notice the rings she never took off – her wedding ring, a ring from her father, and a small pinky ring she received after her own mother's death. Around her neck rests a silver cross necklace. Although my father probably never realized it, she always wore it, only taking it off right before bed.

I can look at her face for only seconds at a time. Her eyes are peacefully closed, which is kind of a deception. I saw her eyes the past few months as she battled cancer. They were not at ease. They were always caught between determination and terror. There were moments when I noticed her kind eyes show through, but these moments were few and far between, and they mostly occurred when Steve and I were in the room together.

Looking at her peaceful demeanor now, I can almost forget just how riddled her insides were with that son-of-a-bitch disease. It still lurks inside, despite her death, adding extra insult. It legitimately offends me. I don't know if I have ever known hate for something as much as I do for the sickness that decided to latch onto *my* mother, and then proceeded to torture her and cause unspeakable pain before ultimately taking her life, all while she was still in her fifties. In moments like these, I understand my brother's rage, and I find myself wanting to rip the cross from her neck.

As my anxiety heightens, I attempt to calm myself with deep breaths. I try to concentrate on five things in the room, that align with my senses, to put my feet back on Earth.

A classic technique from "Dealing with Anxiety 101."

Once I'm back in a "stable" state, I notice Steve is now sitting by Dad. I'm alone up here. He and Dad are purposefully looking the other way to give me privacy. I take the opportunity to look down at her again. After all, this might be it. I shakily reach down, touch her hand, and say, "I love you, Mom. I'm sorry." I know why I said the first thing, but not the second.

I find a seat next to Steve, but I continue to look at Mom. "You ok, Em?" Steve asks. He then shakes his head. "It's so stupid. I feel like that's all any of us ever asks each other, even though we already know the answer."

I begin to cry. Actually, it's not a cry – it's a sob.

"That's my mom."

32

The visitation was scheduled for two hours, but it lasted an additional thirty minutes. Dad stood next to her coffin, followed by Steve and then me. My brother allowed me the final spot, since he knows I'm the most antisocial of the family. Despite Dad's reclusiveness, he is actually able to carry a conversation when he desires – usually discussions about a potential project or one of his famed previous ones – but he did a great job tonight. Probably because he considered this whole thing a job. I think that's what he had to do to not lose his mind. For the first time in a while, I think I actually learned something from him tonight.

Most of the visitors were colleagues, friends, and admirers of Dad's. A few people came to support Steve and me, and that certainly made me appreciate them on a whole new level. I felt less forgotten by the universe when I saw a familiar face, I guess.

After two and a half hours of saying "Thank you," "She was," and "I know," my voice was done for, though. I have not spoken that much since my public speaking class in high school. And, even worse, after two hours of giving awkward hugs, shifting my weight from one leg to the other, and essentially remaining motionless, my body was done for too. I was exhausted and ready to lie down.

After the final person left, Steve and I collapsed next to each other on a pew. We remained silent because moving our mouths was too physically and emotionally exhausting. I expected Dad to collapse even before us, but he didn't. In fact, he remained on his feet long afterward, once again talking to Mr. Underwood. More than that, he was smiling and laughing.

I began to have flashbacks.

"Whatever happened to that job offer of Dad's?" I finally decide to bring up the heated topic to Steve after stewing about it for days.

Steve struggles to follow my line of thinking. "You mean that documentary he talked about at the hospital?"

"Didn't you think he was awfully chummy tonight with some of those people?"

"'*Chummy*'?"

"Specifically, those guys he used to make movies with... like Rusty?"

"Rusty was Dad's best friend for years. He probably still is, if Dad still has what you would call 'friends.'"

"Rusty was his producer."

"Yeah. And they worked together for like twenty-five years. You don't work with someone that long if you aren't friends."

"What about Lucy and Desi? Or Fred and Ethel even."

"Are you talking about Lucille Ball and Desi Arnaz?"

"Of course. *I Love Lucy* was like the biggest show ever."

"That show ran like ten years or something, I don't know. Not twenty-five years. Plus, that was, what, in the 1950s?"

"What has the decade got to do with anything?"

Steve shakes his head, completely flustered. "Are you trying to drive me crazy? What are you talking about?"

I take a deep breath. "Hear me out... I think Dad was wheelin' and dealin' during the visitation tonight." Steve begins to protest, but I stop him. "I mean, look at him. He's still on his feet, with a smile on his face. We're thirty years younger than him and we can't even stand."

"Dad also shot a movie in the Amazon rainforest."

"Why are you defending him?"

Steve scoffs. "I'm not defending him, Emma. I'm just saying... I think you're off on this one. I don't think Dad would do that."

My face immediately squirms. "What evidence do you have to the contrary? That's all he's done his whole life. Use unique opportunities to further his career."

Steve turns and faces me fully, taking on the look of the old Steve that has been gone for days – the one who keeps the family together. "Dad isn't like that anymore. You heard him at the hospital. He would not use *the death of his wife* to try and get a movie made. How would Mom's death even help him?"

"He could use their empathy to work with the best people."

Steve shakes his head. "You're way out of line, Em. Plus, they approached him, remember? He doesn't need to convince anyone to work with him. They needed to convince *him*." Steve turns back, drops his head, and stares at the carpet. "But what do I know about anything? If you're that concerned about his intentions, there's only one thing to do."

"What's that?"

"Go talk to him."

33

I take Steve's advice and approach Dad. Somehow, he is able to smile when he sees me.

"Oh, hey, Em. You guys ready to go?"

I take a moment to gather my bravery. It's not easy calling out a parent about his bullshit. "Yeah, I think so. I… just wanted to ask something before we split up for the night, though."

Dad looks concerned. "What's bothering you?"

"Oh, nothing, it's just…" I take another breath. "Are you making that documentary."

Dad's face contorts as if he smells an unexpected fart. "What?"

"The documentary… you know. The follow-up to *Out of Mind*… Your legacy movie."

"Emma, I told you both at the hospital that…"

"It's just that I saw you tonight talking to all of your old colleagues. Even though they're older, I can still remember their faces. I remember them all because I resented them for years. They used to come to our door and take you away from us, sometimes for months at a time. As a kid, a month felt like a year. So, I have to know… are you doing the movie? Was that what this was all about?"

I can tell Dad is speechless. I'm not sure if it's because I Sherlock-Holmes'd his ass or because he is offended by the very thought of treating Mom's legacy that way. "First off," he begins sternly, "you have no right to accuse me of such a thing." He stops and considers his next words carefully. Perhaps he has learned a lesson or two of his own during this past week. "Or, you know what, maybe you do. Maybe it's not crazy to make an assumption like that. In the past, I was completely career driven. There's no denying that. But look at me," he says, raising up his meager arms that were once so muscular. "I'm old. I'm retired. I don't have a career anymore. I don't have it in me. When I told you at the hospital that I was done, I was telling you the truth. So, no, I am not making the movie. More importantly, *young lady*," he emphasizes, "I would never do that to your mother's memory. You may not believe a lot of what I say... certainly not what I have said in the past. But you can believe that *one* thing."

I have been evaluating not only his words but his speech pattern throughout, trying to detect a lie. I have become quite accurate in detecting his falsehoods. Despite my years of training, or perhaps because of them, I do not detect any dishonesty in my father's words. "Okay," I simply reply.

Dad looks deep into my eyes, as if conducting his own test. "Do you believe me?"

Without a blink or hesitation, I answer, "I do."

Dad smiles weakly. "I am not happy to be here, Em. Except for actually watching your mother die, this has been the worst day of my life, and I know tomorrow will only be worse still. I pasted on a smile for those people because they needed to see that I am strong enough to hold together what is left of our family. After all, most of them know that was your mother's duty for years, because I was a failure at it. I had to show them tonight that I have it in me to make it through – not just for me, but for you and Steve. As hardened as my heart is, even I dislike seeing someone deeply sad. You can't help but reflect upon your own happiness, or lack thereof, when you see someone else in the depths of despair. The only thing worse than seeing someone suffer, though, is seeing a parent suffer. It's hard to watch a father or mother fall apart in front of their kids… to not be strong enough for them. Without your parents, you lose that strongest security blanket that you're swaddled with after birth. Unfortunately, you and Steve just lost a huge part of that security – probably the biggest part, if we're being honest. So I have to step up my game for you guys as well as for myself." He pauses for a breath and reflection. "Does any of this make sense? I feel like I'm rambling."

I smile weakly as well. "It makes perfect sense, Dad."

He nods. "That's why I want you to look after your brother, too. I don't know if you've noticed, but he's falling apart. You've seen his hands, right?"

"He's treating his room like Mel Gibson treats a bad hot tub date. Yeah, I've noticed."

"He's Lucas's dad. We need to make sure Steve stays well for Luke's sake. That boy already has to deal with a split home. He doesn't need to deal with an unstable father who has anger issues on top of that."

"I know," I nod. "You're right. I'll look after him. It's only fair, I guess. He's been looking out for me since the day I was born."

Dad chuckles. "Steve's been looking out for all of us. He's always been…"

"…Kind of the glue," I finish for him.

"Exactly," he agrees. "He's a lot like your mother."

"Please don't say it," I plead.

"And you've always been a lot like me."

I exhale loudly. "A week ago, that would have been the worst insult anyone could have used against me."

"And now?"

"It kinda makes me proud."

34

I toss and turn all night. It has nothing to do with the size of the bed I'm in. Actually, I've grown quite fond of Lucas's tiny bed. I feel as though he may need to find new living quarters the next time he's here. And he can forget about getting Ezekiel back....

I feel as though I have not slept at all, but I know that's not true. I nod off periodically for maybe ten minutes at a time. It is a completely restless sleep, because I immediately enter a dreamscape as soon as I'm out.

I visualize Mom spilling coffee on her new blouse...

I visualize Mom taking that one bite of birthday cake...

I visualize Mom in hospice, gasping for air...

I visualize Mom in her coffin, hands crossed...

I visualize Mom in front of a crowd at her funeral tomorrow.

I am full of anxiety. I don't know what to expect, how to act, or what to say. I know we've been prepped on everything, but those instructions evaporated instantly.

I am sad.

I am nervous.

I am scared.

I just want my mom.

35

"Do you think we'll ever be able to take a normal drive together ever again? You know, one for fun?"

Steve puts the car in park in front of the church. "It'll probably take a while."

"Where's Lucas?"

"Mallory's bringing him after we have the graveside service. It's my day to have him, but she knew I would obviously…" he trails off sadly.

"We'll see him soon."

He hesitates before speaking, but then he decides to actually say what's on his mind. "I'm not sure if that's a good thing or not. Is that wrong of me to say?"

I shake my head. "It's not wrong. He's so young. He can't fully understand what's going on."

"Should I have brought him to this thing?" he asks, pointing to the church. He truly looks lost.

"I think you made the right decision. Let his final memories of Grandma be good ones."

"I guess. I feel bad not having him here, though," he says softly. "I depend on that little guy more than I'd like to admit."

I put a hand on his shoulder. "I know you do. I get it." I give him a couple of pats.

"Hey, Em?"

"Yeah?"

"Please don't pat me like a dog who successfully fetched a ball."

I drop my hand quickly. "Oh, I'm sorry. That wasn't a 'Dat's a good boy' sort of pat… It was more of a 'There, there, don't be sad' sort of pat."

"Do you really think that patting my shoulder will convince me not to be sad?"

"No, not really."

"Then don't do it."

I laugh and he promptly does as well. "What a weird day," I say. "This is so depressing. How can we even laugh?"

"It's what we do," Steve says before falling silent a moment. "This one's different, though."

"It is," I acknowledge.

It takes a moment for him to find his next words. "I know you're worried about me," he says, unintentionally curling his fingers up as he does. "But I'm more worried about you."

"Well, don't be."

"That's my job as the older sibling – to worry. Well, to look after the youngling."

I smile. "I'll be okay, or as okay as I can be."

"I hope so," he says, rather grimly in my opinion. He takes a deep breath and says, "You ready?"

"Let's do this."

Pastor Jacobs ushers us to a back room. Along the way, he gives us some more instructions, which I am unable to latch onto, as well as his well-wishes. The room he takes us to appears to be where the church choir gathers, based on the inordinate number of robes hanging along the back wall, next to a piano. Dad is already seated in the room before we enter.

Before Pastor Jacobs leaves, I pull him aside. "Could you put this inside… you know, with her?" I ask, handing over an envelope.

"Of course," he says. With that, he exits, leaving our family trio to reunite once more.

Dad and Steve kind of eyeball me after I pass off the secret envelope, but neither decides to say anything about it. "So what now?" I ask. I eagerly scan the room looking for some sort of clock.

"We stay back here until it's time," Dad answers calmly. He appears serene. After last night's conversation, I understand why.

"Is it just going to be the three of us?" Steve asks.

"As far as I know." Dad shrugs, and then, as if by comedic cue, we hear a knock at the door. "Come in," he says with reservation.

36

In walks Uncle Terry and his two boys, Brady and Grady. Terry is a straight-up weirdo, and that's not just a family viewpoint. His wife, Leona, left him and the boys ten years ago or so for a man who specializes in squirrel taxidermy down in Branson. Any woman who chooses a squirrel-stuffer over Terry is making a clear statement.

Brady and Grady take after their father. Although they are not conjoined twins, they act as though they are. They can finish each other's sentences effortlessly. Although that's romantic for new lovers, it's simply quite eerie for twin brothers. Adding to their supernatural creepiness are their appearances.

Brady has dark hair, and he wears thick-rimmed glasses and overalls. On the surface, that's not too weird, until you account for the fact that he never wears any other clothes under those overalls, except for, I hope, his underwear. He also wears those overalls every single day – including this one.

Grady has long blond hair and, although he doesn't wear glasses, it would appear as though he needs them based on his squinty eyes. Grady does have a different style of dress than his twin brother, though. He always dresses like Angus Young from AC/DC, in that school boy outfit and hat. Today, he was kind enough to add a tie to his ensemble.

"Jimmy," Uncle Terry says, stalking up to Dad. He grips Dad in in a bear hug that is not reciprocated. He tries to lift Dad up affectionately, but he never leaves the ground. "How are you doing, Buddy?"

"Oh, just great, Terry." Dad then reluctantly adds, "How are you?"

"I'm all right, I suppose. Just had surgery on my foot, so that's slowed me down. Ain't nothing like having a bum wheel, ya know?"

"I can't imagine what could be worse."

Uncle Terry turns toward my brother and me. "Little Em... look at you. All grown up," he says, his eyes lingering a bit too much for my liking. "Hey, Stevie, does Little Em still beat up on you like she used to?"

"I was just a little small for my age," Steve says, nursing the age-old wound.

"You were small for any age!" Terry barks. "You were pathetic. Getting beat up by your sister... your *younger* sister..."

"Yeah, well..." I chime in, a bit too proudly.

"Boys, say hello." Uncle Terry motions to his two automatons.

"Hello, Uncle Jim," the twins say in unison.

"Creepy as ever..." Dad mutters.

"I was surprised I didn't get a call from you, by the way, Jim Stone," Uncle Terry turns his attention back toward Dad.

"Sorry, been a bit busy." Dad's sarcasm meter is off the charts.

"Sure, who isn't this time of year?"

"How did you find out about Annie?"

"Scanner."

"Of course. Still monitoring it like a junior emergency responder?"

"I'm official now." Uncle Terry holds himself up proudly.

"Is that right? They finally gave in?"

"That's right. You're looking at the newest member of the fire department 'slash' emergency response team."

Dad fake ponders. "That's still a volunteer service isn't it?"

Uncle Terry shrugs off the put-down. "They don't accept everyone, ya know."

"Just volunteers."

"Anyway, it's taken a lot out of me. That's how I got this flat tire. I'm lucky I even made it here today."

"To your sister's funeral?"

"I'm in a lot of pain, Gold's Jim."

"Poor you…"

"By the way, I took a look-see before I came back here. She looks *terrible*."

"She's dead, Terry. What did you expect?" Having had enough of Uncle Terry's shit, Dad does the improbable and turns his attention toward his nephews. "How's life going, Boys? Working?"

"I'm working retail," Brady replies with zero emotion. "High position. I practically run the store."

"You must be high if you think you run the store," Dad mutters. Then, more loudly, he says, "What about you, Grady?"

"I've been really busy trying to start up some internet companies. It takes up most of my time."

"Is that so?" Dad is *somewhat* interested.

"What kind of companies?" I ask.

"Have you seen the movie *The Social Network*?"

I answer "No" at the same time Dad answers "Yes."

"Well, Little Em…"

"Don't call me that."

"…err… Well, anyway it's about Mark Zuckerburg, the founder of Facebook."

"He wants to develop a company like that," Brad chimes in.

"Ahh," I say, visibly rolling my eyes.

"Only mine would be more selective," Grady continues. "I want it to be a 'celebrities only' social media app. Only the stars could access it, so they could do whatever they wanted on it. Free from the watchful eyes of the public."

"The court of public opinion," Brady interjects. "You see, celebrities hold back their true feelings and opinions when they use popular apps, like Twitter. They have to maintain an image. They don't want to get canceled. With our…"

Grady shoots his brother a look.

"…*his* app, they can say, do, and post whatever they want, because their audience is strictly other celebrities. It's like we'll be freeing them from…"

"Persecution," Grady nods solemnly.

"Wow, that's fascinating," I reply. Dad tuned out of this conversation the moment Grady said he wanted to be Mark Zuckerburg. Steve was never engaged in this conversation to begin with, so here I am, bearing the weight of it all. "Do you have any other ideas?" I ask after several intensely painful seconds of silence and dead stares from my replicant cousins.

"Well, they all stem from this idea," Grady says. "See as the founder of 'CelebSpace'…"

"That's what he's gonna call it," Brady says proudly.

"I will have access to all of the celebrities who use my innovative app. I will be the only 'normal' guy on there."

"'Normal,'" Dad scoffs. I guess he was listening after all. It's hard to not listen in on absolute train-wreck nonsense, to be fair.

"*And* he'll make it so they can't block him," Brady says.

"So you'll have access to all of the big movie stars… and then what?" I ask. "How will that garner business?"

"I can see what their interests are, and then I'll build ideas around them. 'Oh, I wish someone would cast me as Napoleon in a movie,'" Grady mimics.

"'Oh, I wish there was a vegetarian yogurt shop,'" Brady continues.

"And then *boom!*" Grady shoots back. "I make a Napoleon movie and cast the actor in it."

"Or he sets up a yogurt shop."

"Since they'll want it so bad, they'll help fund it."

"It makes sense," Brady says.

"Perfect sense," Grady admits, smirking at his brother.

"Wow, you've *really* thought about this," I say. "That's super awesome. I hope it works out for you. Not just being an app developer, but also a movie director and architect, I guess." I pause and then add, "I thought yogurt was vegetarian? Do you mean 'vegan'?"

"Most are vegetarian," Brady answers, "but not all."

"You're developing this app yourself?" I can't help but ask. I just have to know how far he has taken this pipe dream. "I'd imagine it's pretty difficult to create and program an intricate social networking app like that."

Grady hesitates, unsure of what to say. He, however, clearly does not want to appear ignorant to us – the "lesser" cousins, whom he and Brady have been in odd competition with ever since they were born. "Yes…" he answers slowly. His voice trembles as he attempts to appear confident. "Yes, I am."

"You hear that?" Uncle Terry says. "My boy's gonna be a trailblazer, just like his Uncle Jimbo."

"That's why I became a filmmaker – to surround myself with the beautiful people," Dad says so dryly that I instinctively look to turn on a humidifier.

"Well, we'll leave it to you then. Big day ahead of ya! If you need anything, be sure to reach out, Slim Jim." Uncle Terry then turns to his boys and clicks his tongue as if his boys were horses that needed corralling. Brady and Grady know the routine, though, and they fall in line behind him at the first click.

As soon as Terry and his nightmares disappear, we are, unfortunately, greeted by more family. This time it is Aunt Roddy and her daughter, Sofia. While we all know it is impossible for Sofia to be as old as her mother, it would still appear as though she were. Their visage reminds me of when a creepy dude sees a mother and daughter walking together and says "Is this your sister?" to the daughter, in hopes that he can score with the giggling mother. Only with Aunt Roddy and Sofia, it goes in the opposite direction.

"Hello, Roddy," Dad greets Mom's other sibling. He seems just as thrilled to see her as he was Uncle Terry. The one upside to Roddy is that, while Uncle Terry is a nonsensical motormouth, Roddy is nearly a mute. She takes after her and Annie's father – Old Man Woods.

Gunner Woods was what you'd expect a man with that name to be. He was born and inbred (kidding) in Missouri, and he only spoke when family members or someone made direct eye contact with him, if someone was discussing classic cars or tractor equipment, or if someone was debating the United States' foreign policy. Much like Cousin Brady, Grandpa Woods also never wore anything other than overalls his entire life. In fact, he was buried in them – the exact same pair that he died in.

On a side note, Steve and I were always told that Grandpa Woods died of a heart attack in the basement of Mom's childhood home. But given the suddenness of his death, the seemingly secretive nature of it, and the odd behavior at his funeral, Steve and I have always believed his death was actually a suicide. Despite being young, even I remember murmurs amongst the adults who said there was a weird spot on the back of Grandpa Woods's head. Supposedly, it was from falling into the wood-burning furnace after falling over from his chest pain. My brother and I, however, firmly believe he stuck a gun in his mouth and blew his brains out that night and remained there until the next morning when his employer sent someone to the house to check on his never-absent employee. We have no evidence to prove that his death was a suicide, other than the fact that maybe he was embarrassed to have produced offspring like Uncle Terry and Aunt Roddy.

"Hello, Jim," Roddy replies. She glances at Steve and me and gives us a solemn nod. Sophia, standing behind her, merely peeks out and makes a grunting noise. I have social anxiety, for sure, but Sophia is on another level. She is essentially a sentient earthworm.

"Where's the 'Maestro' at?" Dad asks.

Roddy's husband, Tommy Antwell, is a composer somewhere in St. Louis. We actually have no idea if he makes a living writing music, but our family has always jokingly called him "Maestro," just to take his pompous ass down a notch. Along with having his nose firmly pointed upward, Maestro Tommy is noticeable for having still-blond hair, despite being in his mid-sixties. Because of that, we have also created a backstory for him that involves his past involvement in the Nazi Party. Even if Maestro were to make an innocent comment about the weather, we will assuredly transform that conversation into a menacing Nazi threat. "Oh, I see zat you are a bit sweaty. Perhaps you would enjoy a nice *shower!*" Steve is the best at creating a fake Nazi voice, always dropping the end of the sentence down a tone so that the threat is real. Sort of like Sherman Klump accidentally turning into Buddy Love when being slightly triggered.

"Tommy is busy preparing a symphony that premieres tomorrow," Roddy replies without humor. "He sends his regards."

"How are you, Sophia?"

More inaudible grunts escape from her mouth.

"That's good."

"We just wanted to pop in before the… festivities begin."

"*Festivities?*"

"Also, I just wanted to mention that I don't do any of this," Roddy says, fake texting on an imaginary phone, "so don't expect me to answer any messages quickly."

"Duly noted," I say dryly. I could not be less devastated.

"So I will see you guys at the next holiday."

"Looking forward to it," Dad says through a painfully fake smile.

"Come on, Sophia."

As Roddy heads to the door, Sophia runs our way and hugs Steve and then me. "You guys are my favorite cousins. I love you guys."

Steve and I share an uneasy glance. Steve is able to be the better person and murmur a "I love you" back. I, however, am physically unable to return her sentiment. I, of course, don't wish any ill will toward Sophia, or any of my family members, but I just can't tell someone I love them if I truly don't feel it. I guess that is a trait passed down from my father.

Pastor Jacobs arrives just in time to end the horror show of Roddy and Baby Jane. "The rest of the family is all seated now," he tells my aunt and cousin. As they scamper off, he turns to us. "We'll wait for the proper music cue and then it'll be your turn to go in. Remember, you'll be on the first row, right side."

"I'll lead the way," Dad says.

As the current song dwindles in the background, Pastor Jacobs asks, "Before we go in, do you mind if I pray with you?"

Steve and I turn to Dad. It's always unclear how he will act in this sort of situation, where a younger male takes the lead. Dad is a lion and he wants to dominate the pride. But today is a new day. It is a different day.

"That would be nice," Dad says. He bows his head first.

Pastor Jacobs prays over us until we hear the music change.

37

I follow Steve, who follows Dad, into the sanctuary. The church appears to be at capacity, which surprises me. I'm not sure why. Maybe I thought Mom didn't get out enough to know that many people. Or maybe because she was my mom, I kind of took ownership over her. It's just another reminder to me, though, of how many lives one person can touch.

After we are seated, Pastor Jacobs begins the service. He first reads her official eulogy. As he reads it, I zone out – not out of boredom, but in sadness. It is hard to hear other people speak those words about her. A song plays after he finishes, but the damage has already been done. I am in a weird, almost hallucinatory, state brought on by intense grief. It's only when the pastor announces my father's name that I snap back to reality.

It's time for the first family member's eulogy.

"I have been married to the same woman for decades. We got together during college and have been together ever since. I went to bed each night knowing that she was going to be there the next morning as my wife. That is, every night until a couple of days ago.

"Looking back, I know I took her for granted. I know I did. I can admit that. I assumed she was always going to be there for me... to escort me through the rest of my life. And now, I understand the hard truth.

"I always chose my career over her. I chose it over my kids, Steve and Emma, as well. I missed their childhoods. I missed their teenage years. I missed their early adulthood. And I also missed Annie's best years. Because, in a guise to provide for my family, I put my self first and my need to be validated by others.

"I still have this visual in my mind... I came home early from a shoot one time, which was a rarity itself, and the family was thrilled. Annie and I vowed we would have a great family night together, playing with the kids on the floor and doing whatever they wanted. After about an hour, though, my back began to ache after weeks of filming in El Salvador and long plane rides. I got up and sat in my recliner. Following suit, the rest of the family found seats as well as Annie turned on a movie for the kids. Once the movie was going, I grabbed my notebook and began mapping out scenes for my next day of filming. I was immediately back in work mode. After writing frantically for a while, I stopped to massage my writing hand. As I did, I glanced over and saw Annie and the kids sitting together – all three of them on the couch. Steve and Annie were fully invested in the movie on the TV, but little Emma wasn't. I spotted her spacing off, her little eyes searching for answers in the void that I had created. When she caught me looking at her, she quickly averted her eyes to the TV. I guess she did it because 'Daddy was working,' and they were instructed not to bother me when that was the case. Deep down, I know, Emma was in some way afraid of me or feared that I didn't love her.

"That night was very telling. The three of them sat together on the couch, while I was sitting off in my own recliner. I was a separate entity from them, as painful as it is for me to acknowledge that now. But Annie never was. Annie was always, first and foremost, Steve and Emma's Mom. As much as I loved my kids, and I did, I was never their father first. And I was certainly never a husband first. I was a filmmaker. The rest of it was all a footnote.

"While I had been a success in my artistic field, I had failed in my life. Just as I was beginning to really come to terms with this knowledge, Annie got sick. The next year was just as fast as it was slow. And then she died. That's when I discovered what real pain was. Living without your constant, your rock, your life's mate… well, I don't know how to do it. I imagine it will take me a while. I just hope it doesn't take me as long as it did to realize that acknowledging you've failed your life's true love is still easier than living without it.

"I'm glad I succeeded as a filmmaker. It was all I ever wanted. But I would give it all back in a second to have her back, even if it were for just another day. Now I realize that's all I want now. Since I can't have that, though, I am dedicating the rest of my life to filling the void left behind by Annie's absence. I will never be as good of a parent or grandparent as she was, but I will give it my best shot.

"My kids and grandchild are my true legacy. Annie knew that all along. Because of her, I know that now, too."

After Dad is seated, the pastor then calls up my brother. Earlier, Steve had asked if I wanted to write a eulogy alongside him, but I declined. Steve is better with words than I am. I barely know how to express myself on a good day, let alone my worst. So, I let him represent the both of us. I knew he would do us justice.

That being said, I couldn't let the day pass without saying anything to her.

I wrote Mom a letter last night before my restless sleep. It was two pages long, front and back. I did not try to be overly profound or poetic in it. I just spoke to her directly, from my heart. I knew no one would ever read it anyway. But it felt good to say goodbye to her when I actually had the time to compose coherent thoughts about what she meant to me.

That was my personal goodbye.

No one will ever hear the words I left for Mom, but they do get to hear my brother's.

38

"In the beginning, in my pre-cognitive state, all I knew was my mother's love. When I think about my earliest memories, Mom was always there. I remember her playing 'Bull' with me, when she got down on the floor and acted as a charging bull while I was, apparently, the world's worst bullfighter. I remember being both scared and excited by the bull when she charged, until she finally tackled me with a swarm of tickles and hugs.

"I can still vividly remember what it felt like to receive one of my mother's hugs. It was an all-encompassing show of affection, filled with incredible warmth. She never gave small hugs – at least until her body began to let her down.

"The feeling I got from her hugs never faded over the years. A mother's embrace is unlike any other. You feel complete safety while in your mother's arms, and that surely has to be because she is the one who carried you to term, bringing you into this world. She knew and loved you first. I love my dad and my sister, but if I heard someone yell out my name, I would most quickly respond to my mother's voice – not just because she gave birth to all eleven-and-a-half pounds of me, but because she would also probably be the first to swat me if I didn't respond.

"Last March, Mom was diagnosed with a critical case of cancer. It was a blow to everyone in the family, but it hit my household in a unique way.

"As good of a mother as she was, my mom was an even better grandma. When Mallory and I told her we were expecting (while playing a rigged game of Password with her and Dad), she screamed in euphoria and nearly took Mallory out of her chair with a hug that could only be replicated by an NFL linebacker.

"Once we were sure that Mallory and the unborn Lucas were okay, Mom quickly decided a few things. She insisted that she be called 'Grandma' because, 'Every kid needs a Grandma.' She also insisted, pending our blessing, upon babysitting her grandson every weekday while Mallory and I worked. We were, of course, thrilled at the idea. Mom watched and spoiled Lucas for the first three years of his life until her cancer just became too much for her to handle.

"I've never seen anyone so devastated as my mom when we finally had to take Lucas away from her during that time. None of us wanted to make the change, but her body was clearly changing. Mom constantly told us she was going to get better and stronger so that she could watch him – or at least share nap times with him again.

"When Mom found out about her cancer last year, one of the first things she said to me, through a flurry of tears, was, 'I don't want Lucas to forget about me.' It's now my life's mission to make sure my son never forgets the love that his grandma had for him.

"Subsequent to nearly fifteen months of doctors' appointments, chemo treatments, and late-night ER visits, our family finally realized that the real end was approaching. After she was admitted to the hospital for the final time a couple of weeks ago, where she also suffered several strokes, Dad, Emma, and I never left her side.

"Watching my strong mother endure a week of hospice care was agonizing. After one major stroke, she lost her ability to speak and nearly all of her ability to respond. At times, she was able to softly grip our hands, slightly turn her head in recognition, or even make a noise that sounded like a chuckle when we said something funny (probably when Emma and I were teasing Dad). But mostly, the only sounds we were left with were moans and short gasps for air. Her breathing became more and more erratic, too. She would often be forced to wait twenty seconds or more between inhaling and exhaling. Each time she did this, it was like watching her take her last breath over and over again. During her last week, I watched my mother die a thousand times, and each time, I desperately prayed that she would be able to take just one more breath.

"Despite the intensity of the situation, I approached every morning with her the same way. Namely, I spilled my heart out to her. I told her how much we all loved her and how she was the heart of our family. I reminisced aloud about old stories and I played her videos of Lucas.

"If you know me well, you probably know that I withhold a lot emotionally. It's tough for me to verbally express gratitude or love in person. And you can forget about getting a hug from me. But I got over a lot of my personal fear in those early morning hours with her. I expressed my extreme anger outwardly, and then I would cry uncontrollably, while holding her hand or stroking her hair.

"At first, I felt bad about expressing my sadness in front of her, because, by all accounts, she was still able to hear us and even slightly respond at times. But I had to be honest with her when I was sad. I am her child. She wanted nothing more than to spare us kids hurt or sadness during her sickness and eventual passing. Because she wanted that, I put on a brave face for her for months.

"Weeks prior, during our weekly movie sessions/visits toward the end of her life, she would occasionally break down and cry as I held her. I was somehow able to muster the strength to hold her up and reassure her that we were all going to be okay. I told her that her case was unique because she was too. As she held onto me, I felt as though our parent/child roles were reversed. I never once cried in front of her during those times. When I went home afterwards, however, I would immediately collapse into Lucas's arms and weep. My little four-year-old boy would hold me up just as I had held my mom up moments prior.

"Once Mom was in hospice care, though, I let all my preconceived notions go. I held her and expressed myself entirely, knowing she'd understand. I was angry at how little time we had left together, so I let my heart bleed out.

"In our lifetimes, we will all lose a parent or a close loved one. There is something specifically horrific, however, about losing a parent. Parents are our life's guide, our safety, and our source of unconditional love. As I write this, I am coming to terms with the fact that I could conceivably live more years without my mother than I did with her. Equally difficult for me is the fact that my son will never see his grandma again, and it has already affected him. He still goes to her door, knocks, and waits until he realizes she's not coming out.

"Emotionally, I feel the same way as my son. I'm still waiting for Mom to come back and surprise me, like this was one of her dark, twisted jokes, but just like my son's knocks on her door, I know my wish will go unanswered.

"It is an impossible task to try to understand why some people have to leave this Earth early, and yet we will always try to make sense of it. I know she is patiently awaiting us in the afterlife. Despite her absence on Earth, though, I know she will live on through our memories, as we await to see her again one day.

"And when that time comes, I cannot wait to hug her once again and feel that warmth that has already disappeared and made my life cold."

With that, my brother leaves the pulpit and returns to his seat.

39

We arrive at the cemetery in a limo provided by the funeral home. I sit in the middle section, while Dad and Steve sit in back. As we turn the corner to where Mom's plot is, my heart sinks even deeper than I thought was possible.

I spot the tent standing in front of her open grave. Some of the funeral home staff members are already stationed beside the tent to seat the family members. On wobbly legs, the three of us exit the car, as if entering a different atmosphere. To us, this is a new world.

We sit in the front row of seats as the rest of the mourners arrive at the cemetery and exit their cars. Everyone is silent. There are no exceptions this time around. Uncle Terry isn't being wacky. Aunt Roddy isn't spewing her pessimism. Dad's former associates aren't popping up with condolences. Everyone is silent, because that's what this moment dictates.

For the memory of Mom.

"'…all go unto one place. All are of the dust, and all turn to dust again,'" Pastor Jacobs concludes the graveside service as the mourners surround him.

The pastor gently closes his Bible. He then walks up to each of us. I am unable to decipher what he says to Dad and Steve. When he gets to me, he takes my hand and says,

"Your mother was a wonderful person with a beautiful soul. I haven't gotten to know all of you that well yet, but I hope I do. I can see just by your demeanor these past few days that your soul is much like your mother's. You have a shell around it, but it is pure and kind. Take care of your dad and brother. And don't forget to care of yourself."

With that, Pastor Jacobs walks away. Some other mourners, including Mr. Underwood and some of his staff, say some pleasantries to us as well, but I know Pastor Jacobs's words will stick with me the most. It wasn't because he was the first to say anything; it was because he compared my soul to Mom's. The highest compliment one could possibly give.

Once everyone is gone, Dad, Steve, and I stand together. We look down at our fourth. Although she's so close, she could not be further away, and I know we all feel that intense pang of loneliness she has left us with. We stand in unison, but we say nothing. We let the silence of the moment do all the talking, with each of us filling in the gaps of a final image we have of her, a final remembrance, and a final goodbye.

Finally, after a few hour-long minutes, Dad says, "You kids ready?"

We nod and begin to follow him when he stops. "You guys go ahead, ok?"

"Sure, Dad," I say. Steve and I exchange a glance and head to the limo. I can't help glancing back over my shoulder, though, just to see what Dad is doing.

Dad bends down in front of Mom's headstone. Because the cemetery is so quiet, I can hear him whisper "Always by your side" as he touches her name.

Unlike the movies, Mom's casket is not lowered into the ground while we are there.

Unlike the movies, we do not each toss in some dirt into her open grave.

Unlike the movies, there is no great speech to cap off this horrendous day.

Unlike the movies, I do not find my purpose in life through her passing.

Unlike the movies, I do not find my final closure by touching her casket one final time.

And that is why I hate movies.

EPILOGUE

Afterlife

Four Months Later

The hours, days, and weeks after a loved one's death feel instantaneously slow and fast. An hour can seem like an eternity. A month can pass in a flash. There is no understanding the nature of time when you face mortality like that.

Every person that we became so close to, or worked alongside with, during that time – Geoffrey the nurse, Pastor Jacobs, Gary Underwood, Mom's doctors, and more – have all gone on with their normal lives. They have certainly already dealt with other deaths by now. Part of me wonders if they even remember us or her anymore.

It is a cliché, but everyone handles death and the grieving process differently. My family is no excuse. We are not back to our "normal" lives. Frankly, I don't think we will ever view our lives as normal again.

Dad and I were most concerned about Steve, given his violent outbursts in the days after Mom's passing. Thankfully, those violent tendencies seem to have died down – at least as far as we can tell – but he is still hurting deeply.

He cries often. He goes to the cemetery constantly – at least once in the morning and once at night. Sometimes, he even makes a midday trip. I don't know what all of his visits are like, but I have gone with him a few times. On those occasions, he always gets down to "her level" and talks about whatever is occurring in his life, no matter how mundane the details can be.

While I feel uncomfortable talking to Mom's burial spot, Steve does not. The end of his visits are consistently the worst. He always breaks down and cries, often hugging her headstone, during his final goodbye. I hate seeing him hurt so much, and I can only hope this intense period of sadness will pass just like his violent phase did.

Outside of the cemetery, Steve is working harder than ever at getting more time with Lucas. Losing Mom has profoundly impacted how he views parenthood. He wants to be as much of a part of his son's life as he can – just as Mom was in ours.

Right after the funeral, Dad immediately returned to his old ways, or at least one of them, and isolated himself at home. He became that reclusive artist that everyone knew and whispered about for years. Day after day, Steve and I both prodded him to get out of the house, to find a hobby, to take a drive, or to just do anything. He refused. Because he's a lion. A lion decides on his own when it's time to hunt, and so does Dad.

After having a lengthy, and what he expected to be contentious, conversation with us, Dad finally agreed to come out of retirement – *one final time* – and direct a follow-up to his biggest film, *Out of Mind*. While his new documentary is still in production, the hype around it could not be greater. The rights to it have already been sold to a major streaming service. All the studio executives needed to see was some footage he had shot with the newly released Eric Davis, and they were immediately on board. "You haven't lost your touch – you're still a legend," is what the congratulatory card actually said.

I could not agree more, and I could not be more proud of him.

As for me, I am not discovering the meaning of life through parenthood. I am not working on a masterpiece that will be admired by millions. I continue to be the underachieving Morris, I suppose.

I, frankly, did not know how to deal with my grief for the longest time. At first, I busied myself with small, minute tasks. I re-hung pictures (by using an *actual* ruler – my house is as symmetrical as a frame from a Wes Anderson film; again, that's Dad's unwanted influence over me), I reorganized everything in sight (including every document and folder on my computer), and I alphabetized all of my books and records (each according to the author's/artist's last name and then by year of chronological release).

It was madness.

After my fidgety stage, I entered an exercise phase. I exercised every day for at least three hours. I lifted weights and ran mile after mile. Much like that day when Mom was in hospice, I found I was pushing myself to unhealthy limits. I lifted weights until my body collapsed. I ran until I got so light-headed I would nearly black out. It was all a distraction. When my body ached, I didn't have to think about the ache in my heart.

I also got really into basketball. It wasn't because I suddenly loved the sport. Really, it was because when I was focusing on perfecting my shot, the voices of torture and remorse finally abated. *Spin it in your hand, flick your wrist, keep your eyes on the rim, and follow through... No time to think about death.* Before I knew it, I was the best shot in mid-Missouri, thanks to two hours of practice every day. Who knew that the key to athletic superstardom was depression?

I'd be lying if I said, "I'm all better now." Just like Steve and Dad, I know I'm not all right. I'm not the Emma I was before. I still exercise too much. I still have OCD decorating tendencies. I do all I can to forget that I lost a person I loved so dearly. Sometimes I don't even realize I'm harming myself, mentally or physically, until it's too late and I self-reflect. But on those occasions, when I know I am about to cross an unhealthy line, I try to think back.

I think that through this whole process, the biggest thing I learned is that life is not about how much money you make or what kind of career you land; it is not about how many acquaintances and lovers you can surround yourself with; and it is not about needing to travel or experience the world to understand it all.

Life is all about the small moments.

The small moments we share with family, friends, or even by ourselves are what allow us to feel we have led a satisfactory life. Those moments could be anything, as long as they are impactful to you.

Playing old records and discussing the meaning of songs with your friends. Reminiscing about, and hearing alternative sides of, old family stories over a holiday dinner while a football game plays in the background. Or maybe taking a walk by yourself in a new city and having a new appreciation for the place you call home. If you accumulate enough of these small moments, I think you can be a happy person.

I think I can be happy.

I have also learned that one person's impact is enormous. I never expected that church to be full on the day of Mom's funeral, but it was. It would not have been full if her influence was negative to those around her. How we impact each other's lives, in big and small ways, has a lot to do with personal happiness as well, I believe.

Overall, I think I grew up being a pessimistic person. I have a dark sense of humor. I can be incredibly selfish. Okay... I am *usually* very selfish. I do not reach out to others, for their benefit or my own, as often as I should. But by acknowledging my faults, I can now work toward addressing them. Personal growth is what they call that, I guess.

In my difficult moments, I think back. I try to think of a small moment when someone impacted me in a greatly positive way. Sometimes I have too many to choose from, and at other times, my mind is so negative I cannot pinpoint one for an hour. The memories are not always the same, but they usually have the same person at the center of them – *Mom*.

The most recent memory is a recurring one, though.

On one occasion, when I was about seven years old, Mom took me with her to go grocery shopping. I *hated* grocery shopping. The only thing of interest to me, or probably any kid, was the cereal aisle, which we always seemed to conveniently bypass. At the end of this incredibly boring shopping trip however, I spotted a book rack.

"Can I go look really quick?"

"Sure. Just make sure you come back when I'm at the register."

I ran to the books and looked them over. At seven years old, I was not a reader by any means, but something drew me to that section. Maybe it was the different colors of the book covers, maybe it was the scantily clad people who donned the covers of some of them, or maybe it was simply the fact that they were the only products in the store that weren't edible. After looking over the entire section, my eyes landed on a comic book. I picked it up and flipped through its colorful pages, enthralled by the images. I then looked over my shoulder and saw that Mom was already at the register, so I ran back.

"Mom, can I get this? Pleeeeeeaaaassseee?"

She looked it over. Her face indicated that she was clearly not a comic book enthusiast.

"I suppose so."

I screamed in delight. I still don't know why I was so excited about that one book in particular, but I was so pumped to have it.

When we got home, and after I begrudgingly helped unload the car, I showed Dad my new comic. He took it from me, flipped through it, and frowned, much like Mom did in the store. Dad, however, came to a different conclusion.

"Throw it away."

My heart was shattered.

"W-why?"

"Because I said so. Go do it."

Dad usually wasn't so short or gruff with us at that age, so his attitude towards me and the book was confusing. Looking back, I still don't know what his issue was. Maybe he didn't want me to see all the violence. Maybe he didn't like the superheroes' skimpy costumes. Or being an artist himself, maybe he just hated the writer or illustrator of the book. Who knows? The end result was the same, however.

After having the comic in my possession for a solid thirty minutes, I took it and gently laid it inside of the kitchen trash can. I then walked away as though my firstborn had been taken from me.

A couple hours later, after the family ate dinner together and had some TV time, Steve and I were sent off to bed. Steve always complained that he shared the same bedtime as his younger sibling, but I think that was all about Mom and Dad checking out after a certain point. Regardless, after we were sent off to bed, that was usually the last we saw of our parents for the rest of the evening.

On that night, however, things went a little differently.

Mom knocked on my door and slowly opened it right after I had gotten into bed. I was happy to see her, because it was comforting to be tucked in by her.

"Emma, can you keep something between just us?"

I perked up in bed.

"Yes. What is it?"

She handed over my comic book. It was still pure, unmolested from any garbage.

"But Dad said..."

"I got this for you. It's okay. He was just being grouchy."

"Are you sure?"

I can still remember her smile.

"Wait until tomorrow to read it, though. It's time for bed now."

I remember that day often for several reasons.

It was a simple day of grocery shopping – something I usually despised.

It was a small thing to let me get a comic book.

Mom's kindness is what stands out – her influence affected me positively. Because of that comic book, I developed a love for reading. Unbeknownst to others, I also developed an interest in writing, although I would never tell anyone that, or even admit to it.

In fact, the closest thing to telling someone about my secret writings was the day of her funeral – when I handed over that envelope to Pastor Jacobs.

Thirty years later, I still remember Mom's small act of kindness and it still inspires me. I think I go back to that memory the most because it has also helped with my grieving.

After she died, I find that I often write about her and how she impacted us – before, during, and after her death.

I know I said I wanted Steve to speak for both of us in his eulogy, and he did a fantastic job. But I think it is important to always hear the words from everyone when you have someone this important in your life.

So this is my book for you, Mom.
Thank you for inspiring me.

"You belong among the wildflowers

You belong somewhere you feel free."

Wildflowers, Tom Petty

Special Thanks

I must first begin this section with a disclaimer – *Wildflower* is a work of fiction.

Yes, this is indeed my most personal book, but the characters and situations presented here are often very fictionalized. The truth is that to write a compelling book, you must introduce a conflict. My novel *Petrarchan Girl* couldn't just be about my main character (Wade Parker) falling in love. He needed additional conflicts to add hurdles to finding that love. In the case of that book, Wade had to deal with a drinking problem and the sadness over recently losing both of his parents. For *Wildflower*, I had to create a conflict within the Morris family. So, Jim became an absentee father who cherished his career more than his family.

In truth, my family is nothing like the Morris family. During Mom's diagnosis and eventual death from cancer, our family remained tight-knit and completely supportive. This is especially true of my father, Chris. He never left my mother's side; he never put his career ahead of her; and he never made my sister or me question his loyalties. He was, and remains, an exemplary spouse and father. The same can be said of my sister. She is my life-long best friend, and she supported me every step of the way during this horrific incident in our lives. I hope I did the same for her.

Because I wanted to be clear that this was a work of fiction, I made the lead character Emma – not Steve. I also made sure to make the first line of the book "I hate movies." Anyone who knows me (or has read any of my other books) knows how difficult that was for me to write. These specific steps were taken to ensure that the reader would know this is a work of fiction.

In fact, the subplot of Jim's documentary filmmaking career was taken directly from the second movie I made. The movie was called *Curmudgeon*, and it featured all of the same Morris family members – Jim, Steve, and Emma – as they dealt with the death of Annie (Jim Morris, one of my favorite characters I've created, also appeared in my novels *The Old Must Die* and *Fearful Farewell*).

The story changed, however, when I faced the real-life death of my mother. The focus of *Curmudgeon*'s story was solely on Jim Morris's filmmaking comeback and how he chose his career over his family. The focus of *Wildflower*'s story is on grieving Annie's death, specifically through the eyes of the children.

Only the trials of real life can shift your focus to what is actually important.

Now, on to the rest.

First off, thank you to my son Dawson for giving me a reason to pull through my own grief, not just during the death of my mother, but also during the writing of this book, which nearly killed me. I love you, Buster. I promised Mom I would never let you forget about her, so that is the biggest reason I wrote this book. I know "Gramma's" so proud of you, and I hope you will forever feel the love she had for you.

Thank you to Dad and Brooke – the only other people who can understand how difficult this book was to write.

Thank you to Aleigha who, unlike Mallory, stuck with me throughout the terrible process of Mom's death.

Thank you to Brogan DeMint for shooting the beautiful picture for this book's cover. It's everything I needed and wanted it to be.

Thank you to my newest collaborator Alyssa Cook for batting clean-up for me. She absolutely came in clutch (and thank you for being a long-time devoted reader as well).

Thank you to Sara Seidel – my most trusted colleague. I needed true objectivity when it came to this story in particular, and she provided me with the guidance I needed – as usual.

Thank you to everyone who supported me, sent cards, and simply talked to me during the difficult past two years of my life. I couldn't have gotten through without those words and acts of kindness. I cannot name everyone, but a few names stand out, including my best friends Chris and Elena, Kirk and Lisa, Joe, and many of my students from over the years, including the class of 2020 who often sent cards and flowers collectively and individually.

And, of course, **thank you, Mom**. I knew you would never read this book, but I still labored over it as though you would. I hope it does justice to who you were as a person and shows the grace, kindness, humor, and strength you possessed your entire life. Thank you for always being there for me, for giving me life, and for endlessly being supportive of my artistic endeavors. You were the first one to believe in me when I wanted to make a movie years ago, and you were the first person to read my earliest book, *The Old Must Die*. I may have lost my biggest fan, but I will always write my books for you. I love you.

Finally, thank you, God. The past two years have not exactly been easy, but my faith in Him got me through my toughest moments. Once again, I know I am not the perfect vessel, but I hope my witness is one that shows a true belief and dedication.

Acknowledgements

Bob Dylan and The Band. "Open the Door, Homer." *The Basement Tapes*, Columbia Records, 1975.

John Lennon. "Grow Old with Me." *Milk and Honey,* Polydor, Geffen, and Capitol Records, 1984.

Tom Petty. "Wildflower." *Wildflowers,* Warner Bros. Records, 1994.

"Take care of all of your memories,

for you cannot relive them."

Bob Dylan

Made in the USA
Middletown, DE
11 October 2022